About the

Elen Caldecott graduated with an MA in Writing for Young People from Bath Spa University. Before becoming a writer, she was an archaeologist, a nurse, a theatre usher and a museum security guard. It was while working at the museum that Elen realised there is a way to steal anything if you think about it hard enough. Elen either had to become a master thief, or create some characters to do it for her – and so her debut novel, *How Kirsty Jenkins Stole the Elephant*, was born. It was shortlisted for the Waterstones Children's Prize and was followed by *The Mystery of Wickworth Manor*, *The Great Ice-Cream Heist* and most recently *The Marsh Road Mysteries*. Elen lives in Bristol with her husband, Simon, and their dog.

www.elencaldecott.com

Check out the **Elen Caldecott Children's Author** page
on Facebook

Also by Elen Caldecott

SPOOKS
and
SCOOTERS

The MARSH ROAD MYSTERIES

SPOOKS and SCOOTERS

ELEN CALDECOTT

BLOOMSBURY

LONDON OXFORD NEW YORK NEW DELHI SYDNEY

Bloomsbury Publishing, London, Oxford, New York, New Delhi and Sydney

First published in Great Britain in February 2016 by Bloomsbury Publishing Plc
50 Bedford Square, London WC1B 3DP

www.bloomsbury.com
www.elencaldecott.com

Bloomsbury is a registered trademark of Bloomsbury Publishing Plc

A CIP catalogue record for this book is available from the British Library

ISBN 978 1 4088 5273 6

Typeset by RefineCatch Limited, Bungay, Suffolk
Printed and bound in Great Britain by CPI Group (UK) Ltd, Croydon CR0 4YY

1 3 5 7 9 10 8 6 4 2

To Bertie and Lily

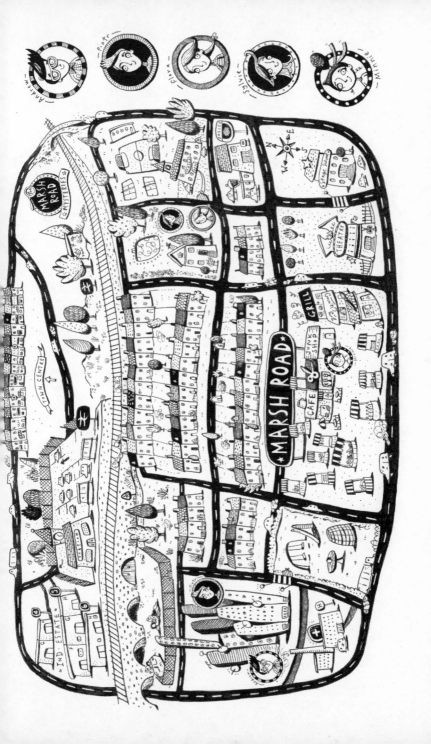

Chapter One

'It's a shame we won't be able to solve any mysteries this half-term,' Flora said.

'When will you be back?' Minnie asked.

'The end of the holidays. We're away for five days, until Friday. But we'll have the last weekend. Maybe, if I'm lucky, there will be a quick fix-it-in-a-day mystery for me to solve with you all before we go back to school,' Flora said hopefully.

She, Andrew, Piotr and Minnie were standing on Marsh Road, outside the cafe. Inside, the cafe looked warm, but out on the street the February wind was freezing. Flora stamped her feet and pulled her duffel coat tighter to stay warm. Around them, the market was quiet; the few shoppers who were there had their heads down and their scarves up. Flora could smell the cold, almost a fog of it.

'It's all right for you and Sylvie,' Andrew said, his

1

spiked hair looking a bit limp in the damp air. 'You're spending the holidays in Tenerife. Where it will be hot. I can't even remember hot.'

Flora smiled. She was looking forward to the holiday, but she would miss her friends. And the chance of solving a mystery.

'Well, if you're lucky,' Minnie said, 'maybe someone will steal the hotel camels, or smuggle rubies across the Sahara, and you and Sylvie can investigate.'

'Have a good time,' Piotr said. 'Send us a postcard.'

'I will.' Flora raised a mittened hand to her friends, then turned and headed home.

It would be nice to spend time with Dad. He was always so busy with work that even when he was around, his mind was often back at Breeze, the company he had founded. His head was so full of bike cogs and scooter wheels and lightweight alloys, and all the bits of people-powered transport they made, it was a wonder his skull didn't rattle. Flora pulled her bobble hat lower, to cover the tips of her ears. In a few hours' time she'd be on a beach with Dad, concentrating on bodyboarding, not board meetings. It seemed impossible!

She turned left into her street. The brickwork of the Georgian terraces was dusty brown in the winter light.

Soon to be swapped for whitewash and blazing sunshine. Flora found herself skipping the last hundred metres to her house. She let herself in.

'Hello!' she yelled. There was no response, though she could hear her mother's voice coming from her study beside the front door. She must be on the phone. Flora pulled off her winter gear – wouldn't be needing that for a while – then ran upstairs to find her twin sister, Sylvie.

She was lounging on her bed. They shared a room and each side of it was as different as was possible. Flora's was neat, Sylvie's looked like an explosion in a charity shop; Flora's bookshelves had books on them; Sylvie's had dance awards and medals. Flora's clothes were tidy – folded neatly on the bed; Sylvie's looked like they had been worn to bed.

Sylvie looked up as Flora came in, but didn't move.

'You should hurry up,' Flora said. 'Dad will be here soon.'

Flora checked her packing one last time. It was done with military precision. Everything was neatly folded and arranged in handy layers – the things she'd need for the first night on top, at the bottom thick jumpers, in case Tenerife in February was not the sun-soaked paradise she was hoping for. A couple of books formed a defensive barrier between clean clothes and germy shoes.

3

Sylvie's case, on the other hand, was a mess. A swim-suit wrestled with a pair of jeans; a blouse had a dress in some kind of headlock, and a wash bag leaked shampoo over it all. The only thing that was packed neatly was the insulin Sylvie would need, and Mum had been the one to pack that.

'You'll be sorry when you get there and everything you have to wear is crumpled and soap stained,' Flora said to her twin, knowing that there was no point at all in giving Sylvie advice.

'Dad will get the hotel to fix it.' Sylvie shrugged. 'Or Anna will.'

Sylvie said 'Anna' in the same way that a nineteenth-century countess might have said 'the kitchen maid'.

Flora pressed her lips together. Ever since Dad had met Anna at Breeze four months ago and they'd started dating, Sylvie had said Anna's name that way. It wasn't fair; Anna was nice. The annoying thing was that she *would* sort out Sylvie's ruined clothes when they arrived. And the chances of Sylvie saying thank you were some-where between zero and nothing.

There was no changing Sylvie though, and Anna didn't seem too upset by it – or at least was good at pretending not to be – so hopefully it wouldn't ruin the holiday.

4

Flora picked an extra book off her shelf and dropped it into her case, just in case she needed to hide.

As she closed the lid, Mum came in.

Flora knew instantly that there was something wrong. Mum cupped her elbows as though she were cold, but her cheeks were flushed an angry red.

'What?' Flora asked.

'Something's happened . . . I'm not sure . . .' Mum's fingers dug into her arms.

'Is it Dad? Is he hurt?'

'No, no. Not that. But he isn't coming,' Mum said, clearly trying to keep her voice under control. 'I just spoke to him.'

Sylvie sprang up like a wounded jack-in-the-box. 'What do you mean, he isn't coming? Why not?'

Mum unfolded her arms and gave a tight shrug. 'He wouldn't say. He wouldn't tell me. He just says he can't.'

'He *wouldn't* say?' Flora could hear her own heartbeat, thumping in her ears. 'Why wouldn't he say?' How could he cancel their holiday and not explain? It didn't make sense.

'I'm not a mind reader. If he won't tell me, how am I supposed to know?'

Flora knew it was disappointment on their behalf that made Mum snap, but knowing that didn't make it hurt any less.

She didn't reply. She sat on her bed and let Sylvie do the ranting.

'Is he going with just Anna instead?' Sylvie demanded. 'Are they going without us?'

Mum shook her head. 'No one's going.'

Some of what Sylvie was saying made it through the confused cloud of Flora's brain – 'he promised', 'planned for ages', 'not fair'. But it was as if Sylvie were talking miles away; mostly all Flora could hear was the blood beating in her ears. A kind of white noise that made her feel dizzy and sick. She felt as if she were crumpling up inside like scrap paper thrown in the bin. She gripped the case full of things she wouldn't need.

'Why?' she whispered.

No one listened. Mum was trying to soothe Sylvie.

'Why?' Flora said louder.

Mum shrugged, her shoulders tight as fists. 'I can't tell you why. He was being evasive. Secretive, even. But . . . well, I do know that he wasn't calling from his mobile. He was calling from his work phone.'

'Work?' Sylvie shrieked. 'Why's he at work when he should be picking us up?'

'Is something wrong at Breeze?' Flora asked before Sylvie could launch herself off again.

'I really don't know, Flora,' Mum said. She paused. 'I'm so sorry, girls. This isn't fair.'

'It must be important,' Flora said. 'He wouldn't cancel for just nothing.'

'Who knows what your father would do for that place,' Mum said sourly.

Mum had never liked the long hours that Dad worked, or the weekends given up to make sure the company he'd set up ran smoothly. They used to row about it a lot.

'Did Dad ask to speak to us?' Flora tried to keep the hope out of her voice, but she couldn't help wondering if Mum had misunderstood. Maybe Dad just meant to postpone the holiday, that they could catch the flight tomorrow instead of today.

'No, he barely had time to speak to me. He said he'd try and see you next weekend.'

Next weekend? At the end of half-term? That was five whole days away! Flora pulled her feet up on to the bed and wrapped her arms around her knees.

'And I don't know what I'm supposed to do now.' Mum checked her watch. 'I took the morning off, but I have to go to work this afternoon. There's a big court case this week; I'm arguing for the defence. I was hoping to get so much done in the peace and quiet.' She sighed. 'I can try and find a temporary childminder, I suppose. I know he's your dad, but Daniel makes me want to scream sometimes, he really does.'

Mum was about to leave when Flora spoke. 'Wait. Can we go and see him, do you think? I mean, at work? He can tell us what's going on. And even if he can't, then we'd be all right waiting there until you've finished. We can read in reception.'

Mum shook her head. 'Dad wouldn't like it.'

'Is that a problem?' Sylvie asked.

For the first time, a flicker of humour flashed across Mum's face. 'It's tempting, but it wouldn't be fair on you. If there's some big crisis at Breeze then no one will look after you properly.'

'Mum,' Flora said firmly, 'Dad should give us a proper explanation. And we'll be safe there. You won't have to worry about getting someone to look after us at the last minute.'

Mum wavered for a minute. She checked her watch

again. 'All right. He said he was rushing to a meeting, but I'll call reception and make sure they get a message to him. I'll drop you there on my way to work. We'll leave in fifteen minutes. I'm so sorry this has happened, girls, I really am.'

Flora stood and gave Mum a hug. She felt Mum's arms wrapped around her, warm muscle and cashmere. She heard Mum swallowing a sob. Mum hated to see them hurt. Flora hated to be hurt.

So whatever secret Dad was keeping, it had better be a matter of life and death.

Chapter Two

They drove in silence. The mood of the day had changed so completely. Sylvie, next to Mum in the front of the car, seemed wound up tight. Flora felt the same way. The excitement of checking and rechecking her passport that morning seemed like forever ago.

The streets outside glided past. In the warmth of the car, Flora was cocooned from the cold. Part of her wished they could just drive around and around, watching the town, without having to get out, ever.

But all too soon, Mum drew up outside Breeze. The company had offices and a big workshop on the industrial estate. The front part of the building was red brick and squat. The back part was a big green steel construction. The two halves were connected by a glass atrium and a long corridor, but she couldn't see that from the front. If she squinted, Flora thought the building looked a bit like a stranded turtle.

The engine idled.

'Do you want me to come in with you?' Mum asked.

'No,' Flora said, 'we'll find Dad and wait with him until you finish work. It will be OK.' She'd never got used to reassuring Mum, though it happened quite often.

'Fine. I don't think I really want to see him today. I'm not sure my tongue would stay civil. I'll call some childcare agencies for tomorrow. Your dad, he – oh.' Mum made a frustrated noise, as if words were no good for explaining just what Dad was.

'I know,' Flora said. 'We'll see you later.'

'Bye, Mum,' Sylvie said.

The temperature outside the car was enough to make Flora shiver, despite her duffel coat. She tugged her hood up over her bobble hat and pulled on her backpack.

She waved as Mum drove off with a toot of the horn.

Sylvie hadn't waited; she was already pushing open the door to Breeze.

Flora followed her inside. The usually calm reception area now looked like a scene from a shouty daytime talk show with security guards holding back the audience members. It was nothing like a regular Monday. The

11

reception and the panic-stricken receptionist were surrounded by flapping people in suits – their mouths flapped, their hands flapped, their many manila folders flapped. No one was listening to a word anyone else was saying.

Not a single person looked around at their entrance.

She could feel Sylvie bristling like a grumpy hedgehog beside her. Being a twin, a living game of Snap, she was used to being noticed. Being a young actress, she *demanded* to be noticed.

Being ignored was not, at all, acceptable as far as Sylvie was concerned.

Flora didn't mind, though. It gave her time to try and work out what was going on. If Dad was at Breeze instead of collecting them to take them to the airport, then whatever had happened had to be related to the company. And the chaos of reception only bolstered that impression.

Flora glanced around for clues. Some of the very best Breeze products hung down from the ceiling, lit by spotlights, like exhibits in a museum. The bike that had won the Tour de France; a stunt skateboard that had been in a famous music video; a slimline scooter that had been the most-wanted Christmas present three winters ago – they'd run out of stock at one point and fights had broken out between desperate parents. The white walls looked as crisp as ever; the supersize sofas in primary colours looked as cheerful as they always did.

So why were the people at the desk yelling?

She and Sylvie moved closer.

The receptionist was trying to answer three phone calls at once – as soon as she said 'Hold, please' into one receiver, another one rang. She scribbled on a Post-it note and stuck it on the countertop with dozens of others.

Flora could make out some of the words being yelled: 'How did it happen?'; 'Drillax are moving fast'; 'Industrial espionage!' Interesting. They needed to speak to Dad.

She wondered how she might get the receptionist's attention. She raised her hand slightly, as though she were in class. Then she lowered it again, feeling stupid. She wasn't sure what to do.

Sylvie, on the other hand, did. She barged through the small crowd, all elbows, until she was at the front. She laid both palms carefully on the counter, avoiding the jigsaw of Post-its. 'I'm Sylvie Hampshire. This is Flora.' She pulled Flora through the scrum to the desk. 'We're here to see Daniel Hampshire. Our dad.'

The receptionist blew her fringe out of her eyes and focused, for a second, on Sylvie. 'Oh, yes, your mum said

13

something . . .' She picked up Post-its and let them drop like confetti. 'But I haven't . . . well, wanted to disturb them.'

Sylvie raised an eyebrow.

The receptionist sighed. 'I'll try my best,' she said, and reached for a phone.

Flora's gaze dropped towards the scatter of notes while the receptionist made the call. She knew it was wrong to read private messages. But messages stuck to the countertop weren't private, were they? They were out in the open, almost public property. She squished the voice that told her they were only there because there was no room left beside the phone. Squished it flat. And tried to read upside down.

It was tricky. Especially as the receptionist had handwriting worse than an inky spider tap-dancing on paper.

But she could read the odd word: *spy*, *theft*, *5000*, *stolen*.

Spy? The disappointment that had draped the day shifted slightly and a tiny glimmer of light shone through. Could this be a case? What had been stolen? Was this what Dad was so reluctant to reveal? Five thousand of what?

She tried to get closer to the notes.

'Flora!'

The voice calling her name made her jump back, more than a little guiltily.

'Flora! And Sylvie too.'

It wasn't her dad. She turned to see Anna, Dad's girl-friend, standing by the reception desk.

Anna smiled tightly at the receptionist. 'Thank you, Mabel, I'll take it from here.'

Anna looked like someone faced with a surprise test she hadn't revised for. Her dark hair was escaping its ponytail. Her light brown skin had not a single drop of make-up on it. But then, Flora had seen her spend a whole day in a top that was on inside out, so it wasn't that odd.

'This is some kind of a day, isn't it?' Anna asked.

'Where's Dad?' Sylvie said.

'Hello, Sylvie,' Anna said smoothly. When they'd first met her, Anna had said that it would be tricky to tell them apart, but actually, she'd got the hang of it quickly – Sylvie was the one scowling at her.

'Hi, Anna,' Flora replied. For them both.

'It's awful about the holiday, isn't it?' Anna said. She moved away from the clamour of the desk and settled down into a yolk-yellow sofa. She patted the seat beside her and Flora sat down. Sylvie balanced on an apple-red cube.

'Where's Dad?' Sylvie asked again.

Anna's smile faltered. 'He's a bit caught up at the moment. He's in . . . he's with . . .'

'Is he all right?' Flora asked. 'What's happening?' She was certain now that there was a problem at Breeze; she couldn't shake off the worry about Dad.

Anna swivelled to face her and laid her hands gently on Flora's shoulders. 'I can't tell you too much, but I promise he's going to be fine.'

Going to be? That meant he wasn't now.

'I want to see him!' Flora said.

'Me too,' Sylvie added.

Anna dropped her hands into her lap. 'You can't at the moment. But you can stay with me until he's free.'

'When will that be?'

'I'm not entirely sure. Listen, why don't you come through to the offices and let me see if I can find some tea or squash or something.' She stood up and walked back towards reception.

Flora made to follow Anna. Then she realised Sylvie hadn't moved. 'What?' she asked.

'I don't want her, I want Dad,' Sylvie replied.

'Me too. But listen, there's something going on. Everyone's working hard to keep it a secret. But if Dad's

16

in trouble, I want to find out what it is. The best way to do that is to be nice.'

'Nice?' Sylvie managed a weak smile. 'If I'm nice, will I get my holiday back?'

'Come on, let's find out.'

Anna buzzed them past reception with her badge. Inside, the hectic atmosphere was worse. People flew across their path, ducking into the offices, whispering, holding rafts of paper and phones and tablets in front of them like talismans to ward off evil. It smelled of burnt coffee, deodorant sprayed too heavily, floor cleaner. It was Dad's world. And she and Sylvie weren't part of it.

'This way,' Anna said. She led them into a big office, with five desks spaced around some tall plants. Light was sliced by blinds as it came into the room. 'This is mine,' she said, pointing to a desk in the corner. 'I'll find some chairs.'

No one so much as looked at them; everyone tapped furiously at keyboards and read the scrolling texts on their screens. Anna went to pinch a couple of chairs from an empty desk.

'I don't like her looking after us like this,' Sylvie whispered.

'You don't like anyone. Except for Piotr,' Flora replied. Flora knew that Sylvie was a big fan of Piotr's, though she

17

would never tell him so to his face. Sylvie was less keen on Andrew, who was more of a drama queen than she was herself. And she couldn't stand Minnie, the last member of the gang, who made it clear that she didn't much like Sylvie either.

Anna wheeled two chairs towards them. 'Sit. Can I get you a drink?'

They shook their heads.

'Anna,' Flora said, taking a seat. 'Please tell us. Why has Dad cancelled the holiday?'

'I can't really . . . it isn't my place . . . Your dad will explain, I'm sure. Probably.'

Sylvie sat reluctantly, as though the chair might be pulled out from under her.

'We'll just have to entertain ourselves while we wait for him to be free. I could set you up on my computer. Or I've got some books in my suitcase. It's just under the desk. I was on my way to the airport when your dad called. So . . .' She tried to force a smile. 'I remembered to pack *The Lion, the Witch and the Wardrobe*. Any takers?'

It was the book they'd been reading at Dad's house. Anna's favourite. She even had a cat called Mr Tumnus. Flora thought it was nice that she'd thought to bring it on holiday. Not that they were going on holiday.

'That's boring,' Sylvie said. She crossed her arms. 'I'm not staying here all day. I want to see Dad and I want to see him *now*.'

'I'm afraid you can't,' Anna said softly.

'How exactly will you stop me? Pile paperbacks on top of me so I can't move? Come on, Flora.' Sylvie stood and walked out of the door without a backward glance.

Chapter Three

Flora gave Anna an apologetic smile but followed Sylvie out of the office.

'Wait for me!' Flora said. Sylvie's coattails flapped like banners as she stalked down the corridor. She didn't even slow down. 'Wait! You're going the wrong way!'

'Oh.' Sylvie stopped. She looked back at her sister. 'I thought this was Dad's office?' She pulled open a door. It was clearly a broom cupboard. With a man standing in it. He wore a suit and was staring at the dusters with his phone held loosely in his hand.

The day was only getting weirder.

'Hello,' Sylvie said. 'Why are you in a cupboard?'

The man sniffed and wiped his nose with a hanky. 'I just needed a moment alone,' he said finally.

'Oh. Why?'

The man didn't reply.

'Do you want me to leave you to it?' Sylvie asked.

'Unless you need cleaning products right now, I would appreciate it,' the man said.

Sylvie shut the cupboard.

'OK, smarty-pants,' she said, turning back to Flora, 'which way is it?'

They'd only been past reception a handful of times in the past, and never unaccompanied, but Flora was pretty sure she knew the way. Dad's office was near the atrium, the big glass hall that divided the offices from the workshop. There was a kind of balcony with big meeting rooms that ran around it. Dad was there, somewhere.

They found a staircase, its pale wood dotted with steel buttons. They padded up softly, not wanting to be stopped.

At the top, they saw a door marked *Daniel Hampshire, Managing Partner*. The door was closed.

'Should we knock?' Flora whispered.

Sylvie reached up and rapped smartly on the wood. Then, without waiting for an answer, she turned the handle and went inside.

Three people inside the room turned to look at the door. Two looked angry, one looked astonished. Dad.

'Sylvie? Flora?' he said softly. He sat at his desk. His

21

white shirt looked as though it had been pulled out of the ironing basket without ever meeting the iron. His face did too. His skin had the grey, wrinkled look of a book that had been dropped in the bath.

'Dad? Are you OK?' Flora asked, creeping into the room.

Flora glanced at the other people with Dad. She recognised them from the handful of times she'd been to Breeze before: Janyce Penning and Tony Valeti, two of Dad's partners.

Janyce placed her hands on her hips. Her red nails looked wicked against the black of her suit. 'Daniel, this is no place for children today. Not even yours.'

Dad nodded wearily. 'I know, Janyce. But we were meant to be on holiday.'

'It's not a day for holidays either!' Janyce replied.

Sylvie ignored Janyce, as though she hadn't spoken. She rushed straight to Dad and gave him a quick peck on the cheek.

Tony sighed. 'Daniel, I'm sorry, but Janyce is right,' he said. He looked as though he had been called in from home – he was in jeans and a rugby shirt. Only his expensive signet ring made it look like he was in charge of anything.

Flora decided she didn't like either of Dad's partners very much. She knew he had a third one, Bruce. She was glad he wasn't there to bully Dad too.

Flora moved across the room so that she and Sylvie were either side of his desk, like lions guarding gates.

Dad's blue irises looked watery, his eyes bloodshot. Flora reached out and touched his hand. Dad's fingers felt rough, hard, but they curled carefully around Flora's palm.

He looked like he needed a hug.

So Flora gave him one.

'Are you OK?' Flora whispered again.

Dad sighed. 'I will be. I'm so sorry about today. The holiday.'

Sylvie broke in. 'What's going on? What happened to Tenerife?'

'I can't say,' Dad said, 'just a bit of bother.'

'That's the understatement of the year,' Janyce snapped.

'Something to do with Drillax?' Flora guessed, remembering what she'd overheard in reception.

Dad recoiled, shocked. 'What do you know about Drillax? No one is supposed to know.'

Janyce threw her arms in the air. 'This is a PR nightmare!' she said. 'The Breeze 5000 leaked and everyone knows about it. Even infants!'

'We're not infants,' Sylvie said sharply.

'Well, you're not one of the only four people in the world who were supposed to know about it!' Janyce replied, equally sharply.

'Janyce!' Dad snapped. 'That's my daughter you're talking to.'

Janyce's mouth pressed more firmly closed than a clam with anxiety issues.

But Tony was backing her up. 'Daniel, the girls can't be here. Walls have ears, as we've learned to our cost this morning.'

'I haven't said a word to anyone!' Dad insisted.

'I know, I know, I never said you did.' Tony held up his palms. 'We'll get to the bottom of this. The private investigator is on his way. Bruce says he's very good, used him when he divorced his fourth wife.'

'The police might be better,' Dad said.

'Daniel!' Janyce hissed. 'Can we have this very sensitive conversation in private, do you think?' She looked pointedly at Flora's hand, still clasped in Dad's.

The door opened again. Janyce sighed in exasperation.

Anna stepped in. 'I'm sorry, I know you don't want to be disturbed,' she said quietly. 'I was looking for the twins. Oh. Sorry.'

Dad smiled at Anna. The look on his face was like nothing Flora had seen before. It was as though Anna was the sun and he was a flower unfurling. For the first time, he didn't look so tired.

Flora felt her own chest tighten. 'We'll go with Anna,' she said to Dad. 'We'll see you later.'

'Yes,' Dad said, 'I'll explain everything as soon as I can.' He looked grim. 'I'm a long way from finished.'

'We sincerely hope so,' Tony agreed.

Flora gave his hand one last squeeze, then grabbed Sylvie's arm and followed Anna from the room.

Her mind was reeling.

Dad was keeping secrets.

Janyce was freaked about a leaked 5000.

The same 5000 that was on a Post-it in reception?

And who were Drillax that Dad was so frightened of?

It was time to get the gang together.

Chapter Four

Anna took them back to her office. They were all subdued now, hardly speaking. The girls sat without having to be told.

'I think we could do with something to perk us up,' Anna said. 'Wait here. I mean it. *Here.*' She pointed at the chairs.

Flora nodded.

The other people in the office had their heads down, crouched over their keyboards. Everyone was on edge.

Flora wheeled her chair closer to Sylvie's. 'I want to go and talk to Piotr and Minnie and Andrew,' she whispered.

'Why?'

'Because Dad needs our help. There's a mystery at Breeze.'

Sylvie didn't look convinced.

'I'm right,' Flora said. 'We need to get out of here and find the others.'

Anna returned with three steaming mugs and a jar on a tray. 'Hot chocolate. I even found some mini marshmallows to go on top. Do you like marshmallows?'

Flora nodded. She did want to leave and find Piotr, but she couldn't bring herself to be impolite.

Anna unscrewed the jar and sprinkled white and pink blobs into the chocolate.

'Thanks,' Sylvie said. 'A few more, please.'

'I suppose sugar is good for shock,' Anna said. 'And today has been full of shocks for you.'

Flora sipped. The sweet, melting mallow pooled on her tongue. It reminded her of Sunday mornings at Dad's, of him frying bacon at the stove, then a walk in the woods, or along a sculpture trail, then hot chocolate in a cafe to warm up afterwards. Dad teasing her about her pink cheeks matching the pink sweets. Suddenly, Flora was horribly certain that she was going to cry. She gazed up at white ceiling tiles.

Anna passed her a tissue in silence.

Flora wiped her eyes and took another sip of her drink. She wouldn't cry. It was better to do something than to mope.

It was just that it would have been so nice to spend time with Dad. Holidays were their one chance to get used to him being around; when they didn't need to plan day trips, or work out timetables and agendas or things to do, the way they did at weekends. On holiday, they could just *be*.

'I'm sure Daniel will rearrange the holiday,' Anna said kindly.

'It isn't that! I don't mind about not going away,' Flora said.

'I do,' Sylvie said.

'I just wanted to see him, that's all.'

'He has to stay. He has no choice.' Anna squished at the marshmallows in her cup with a spoon, pressing them against the white ceramic. 'I'm sure he'll take you away somewhere once all this has blown over.'

'When will that be?' Sylvie asked.

'I'm not sure.'

'It won't be this half-term though, will it?' Sylvie said.

Anna sighed. 'I guess not.' She looked at them sadly.

'What's the Breeze 5000?' Flora asked. She peered at Anna as innocently as she could.

Anna's eyes widened. She glanced quickly at the other

people in the room. 'Where did you hear that name?' she whispered.

'In Dad's office.'

'You really shouldn't know about it. No one should. Hardly anyone did before this morning.'

'Is it a new invention?'

Anna bit her lip. She looked frightened. 'We really can't talk about it.'

'But it's been stolen?' Flora asked.

'The blueprints have,' Anna admitted.

'Drillax?' Flora guessed.

'Hush!' Anna insisted. 'You can't say that name in here. Not today. Not at all.'

Flora itched to start investigating. Who were Drillax? What had they to do with stolen blueprints? What had they done to so upset Dad?

'Your dad really wouldn't want you to get involved,' Anna warned. 'There's a private investigator on his way. You two should just stay put. Shall I find something for you to watch on the computer?'

This was the exact opposite of what Flora wanted. She looked at Sylvie, who still looked grumpy. How could they get out of Breeze and find the others?

Sylvie shrugged. She wasn't going to help.

'You don't need to watch us,' Flora said. 'We could go and see our friends; we're just in the way.'

Anna laughed. 'You're not in the way. I'm supposed to be on holiday, remember? All my work is up to date. Although there's probably something Janyce wants me to do for the big anniversary party at the end of the week.'

'Won't they cancel the party? If the company is in trouble?' Sylvie said.

'It isn't in trouble!' Anna insisted. 'It's just got a few bumps in the road, that's all. And the party has been planned for months, to celebrate ten years of Breeze. Of course they won't cancel. It would look really bad if they did. It will all get sorted, don't worry.'

Anna scooted herself over to her computer. There was a picture of her brown-and-ginger tabby cat in a frame beside her desk. His face was squished right up to the camera in a way that made it look like a paparazzi shot. Flora noticed a second photo, one of Anna and Dad on a beach together. Laughing at the camera. She didn't recognise the scene. She and Sylvie hadn't been there. She wondered who had taken the photo. The two photos were the only decoration Anna had. Other than that, there was only the big computer screen on her desk. Anna wiggled her mouse and the computer lit up.

'I'll just check my emails, then I'll find you a cartoon or something.'

Sylvie rolled her eyes at the suggestion of a cartoon.

Even Flora winced.

She looked towards the door. Could they sneak out without Anna noticing? She was pretty forgetful, but Anna probably would remember that she was meant to be watching them. Maybe a diversion, then? That might work. She put her empty mug down on the tray. She felt stronger now, ready to act.

'Oh.' Anna made a noise that was half cry, half moan.

Flora looked at her. Anna's skin wasn't warm brown; it had turned an ashy pale, as though there was no blood in her cheeks at all. Flora noticed that Anna's fingers were trembling above the mouse. 'Anna? Are you OK?'

Anna clicked rapidly with the mouse, like a shooting game. She closed the screen. 'Fine, fine. Absolutely.'

She didn't sound fine.

'What's wrong?'

Anna forced the brightest, cheeriest smile. It got nowhere near her eyes – they flicked back to the screen. 'Nothing, nothing.'

She stood up.

Then sat.

Then stood again. 'Would you two be OK if I nipped out for a moment?' she asked.

'We don't think we're going to wait, actually,' Sylvie said. 'We're going to Marsh Road, to see Piotr.'

'Marsh Road?' Anna said in a whisper. She was still staring at the blank screen.

'Yes, to see Piotr. Will you tell Dad for us?' Sylvie was already out of her chair, heading towards the door.

'Marsh Road,' Anna repeated robotically.

'That's right.'

Flora stood up with a scramble. This was their opportunity to go. Anna was obviously distracted. Sylvie was already out of the door. This was what she wanted, wasn't it? A way out?

But not with Anna looking so upset. It felt wrong to leave her, so, so . . . Flora wasn't sure how to describe the way Anna looked.

'Flora!' Sylvie's head popped back into the room. 'Come on, if you're coming.'

'Bye, Anna,' Flora said reluctantly, and followed her sister.

Anna still stared at the screen.

In the corridor, Flora glanced back at the door to Anna's office. 'Was she all right, do you think?' she asked Sylvie.

'Of course. Except for thinking we'd want to watch *Peppa Pig*, there's nothing wrong with her. You know her head's in the clouds most of the time.'

But, Flora thought, if it wasn't for the fact that Anna was a grown-up, and Dad's girlfriend at that, she could have sworn that Anna looked frightened.

They had to reach Marsh Road and get help from the others.

Chapter Five

'Should we tell Dad we're leaving?' Flora asked Sylvie.

'No. Let Anna tell him.' Sylvie shrugged.

They were near reception, about to go through the door into the public area. They could still hear phones ringing madly. Nothing had calmed down in the slightest.

Especially not Sylvie, Flora thought.

'Why are you being so cross?' Flora asked.

'I'm not cross. Why should I be cross just because Dad cancelled our holiday, then wouldn't tell us why, then told his soppy girlfriend to look after us because he was too busy? And then have that soppy girlfriend get so super soppy she can't actually look after us properly anyway? Why should any of that bother me?'

Sylvie leaned hard against the door and, stepping out into the reception area, let it swing closed behind her.

Flora's hands shot up, to stop the door hitting her in the face. 'Sylvie!'

But Sylvie ignored her. She stalked out of reception into the street.

'Wait!' Flora trotted after her. When she finally caught up, she realised that Sylvie's eyes were glistening dangerously. She dropped into step beside her twin. Trying to get her to talk would be a very bad idea. Sylvie was liable to lash out when she was angry.

Marsh Road market wasn't far. But the buildings and warehouses on the industrial estate seemed to form wind tunnels. Freezing flurries of air whipped past them. They walked in a spiky silence. Flora felt her eyes watering again, this time from the cold. Then they turned down by the railway arches and followed the footpath on to Marsh Road.

The market was sheltered a little from the weather. The shops and houses on either side were a buffer against the gusts. The odd yellow leaf had settled on the stall canopies, clinging damply to the striped plastic awnings. The traders today were wrapped up for the weather – fingerless gloves and scarves, their cheeks made rosy by cold.

The cafe, where the gang usually hung out, was warm in comparison. The glass door had steamed up, so that it was impossible to make out the people inside. Flora pushed it open and immediately unbuttoned her duffel coat – it was like a sauna.

Piotr and Andrew were there, sitting in the window seat. Minnie was at the counter, chatting to Eileen and Katie, who owned the cafe. Flora sidled up to her and patted her on the arm.

'Flora!' Minnie gasped. 'Aren't you on a plane?'

'Evidently not,' Sylvie said behind them.

'It's a long story,' Flora said.

Minnie gave a lopsided, sympathetic smile. 'Come and tell us.'

Minnie led the way over to the table where the boys waited. Andrew, his glasses a bit misted from condensation, nearly bounded out of the seat when he saw them. Piotr looked worried.

'Andrew,' Minnie snapped, 'don't climb on the furniture.' She was taller than the others, which sometimes made her behave as though she had to keep Andrew under control. Not that anyone could.

Piotr's eyes looked concerned under his flop of mousy fringe. 'Is everything OK?' he asked. 'Why aren't you on the beach?'

Sylvie slid into the booth. 'Cancelled,' she said, shrugging.

'Postponed,' Flora said.

'I'm sorry,' Piotr said, 'why?'

'Dad's in trouble,' Sylvie said. 'We have no idea why.'

'That's not quite true,' Flora said. 'We've just come from Breeze, where Dad works. It's all a bit chaotic there this morning, but we've got a good guess what's going on.'

'Have we?' Sylvie asked in surprise.

'Yes, of course. And we need your help.'

'Do we?' Sylvie said.

Flora reached for her backpack. She always carried it everywhere, and inside was an empty notebook. She'd been planning on using it to make a scrapbook of their holiday – bus tickets and cafe receipts and museum entries, all the things that would remind her of being away with Dad.

Instead, it was going to be their case file.

'Right,' Flora said, 'here's what I know about the case so far. At some point recently, Dad has been working on something called the Breeze 5000.'

'What's that?' Andrew asked.

'That's one of the things we don't know,' Sylvie said.

Flora shrugged in reluctant agreement. 'The Breeze 5000 is top secret. Only a very small group of people know about it at all.' Flora looked around the cafe. Most of the tables were full and there was a constant chatter that masked their conversation from prying ears. 'Well, from what we overheard, I suspect that somehow, a company called Drillax got their hands on the blueprints, and now it isn't secret any more.'

'So what?' Andrew said. 'Their secret's not secret any more. They'd have to talk about it sometime, otherwise how would anyone know it was for sale?'

Minnie rolled her eyes towards the yellowing ceiling. 'Andrew, if another company can make a product without having to pay to test it and trial it and do all the work, then they can sell it cheaper than Breeze. No one will buy Breeze's version.'

Andrew pushed his glasses further up his nose as he considered this. Then he said, 'I bet whoever lost the blueprints is in massive trouble at Breeze. I bet they're getting the telling-off of their life.'

'Janyce said they were leaked, not lost. Breeze are bringing in a private investigator to find out who leaked the plans,' Flora said, 'but for now the company is in uproar. No one knows what to do.'

'That's industrial espionage!' Piotr said in wonder.

'Oh! Spying! Who's the spook?' Andrew asked.

'Spook?' Minnie said.

Andrew rolled his eyes. 'Don't you watch any Sunday afternoon films?'

'Black-and-white movies about war? No, not really.'

'Well, you should. They're educational. Basically, I've learned never to trust the man with the posh accent. Spooks are spies, secret agents; it's also another word for ghosts, of course, but I don't think that's relevant here.'

Flora felt a shiver travel up her spine. There was a spook at Breeze. Someone who had betrayed everyone there. And they had no idea who.

'So,' Andrew said with a grin, 'we're going to track down a spook.'

'Are we?' Piotr asked.

Andrew nodded. 'Of course we are. If the spook has stolen once, they'll do it again. If Drillax steal all their products there will be no Breeze left.'

Flora felt cold again, despite the steam. Breeze was Dad's whole world.

'We might never get our holiday!' Sylvie said.

Minnie clicked her tongue at Sylvie.

'Dad can't lose Breeze,' Flora said. 'It means everything to him. Maybe even more than us.' She said the last part very quietly, muttering over the clatter of washing up and cutlery scraping plates. It wasn't something she even

39

wanted to admit. But she knew it was true. Breeze was the most important thing in Dad's life, Mum always said so.

She couldn't bear for him to lose it.

She looked down at the tabletop. The plastic was speckled grey and brown, so as to disguise the splashes. The specks wavered and warped as she stared at them. She rubbed her damp eyes and the pattern settled back down again.

'How can we catch a spook?' Andrew asked.

'I don't know,' Flora said.

Piotr unwrapped a Kit Kat thoughtfully, tearing through the silver foil with his thumbnail before snapping up the sections and passing it around. 'The first thing we need to know is where the blueprints were stored and who had access to them. The second thing is who are Drillax and how did the blueprints get into their hands? How can we get information about the comings and goings inside the factory?' he asked.

Flora took half a finger of chocolate. Then, she smiled and said, 'Anna.'

Chapter Six

Flora was sure that she could persuade Anna to help them. To help Dad. She felt a little brighter already – she often did when she'd made a decision and wasn't just moping.

'Will we go and find her now?' Andrew asked. 'If we go to Breeze, will they let me have a go on that bike that Bradley Wiggins used?'

Flora shook her head. 'No, famous ones are stuck to the ceiling.'

'Oh. Shame.'

Flora wondered whether it was a good idea to go straight back to interview Anna now. She'd seemed so odd when they'd left her, so distracted. Maybe it was better to let things calm down a bit. 'I think perhaps we should go back in the morning,' Flora said finally. 'Anna might have more information for us then, anyway. She was a bit weird, to be honest.'

Sylvie made a snorting noise.

Flora heard her phone buzz – a message. She rummaged in her bag until she found it. A message from Dad!

Where are you two? With Anna? Am worried. Reply.

Oh. Anna hadn't passed on their message. She really was more distracted than usual. Flora texted back quickly, so that Dad would stop worrying.

With Minnie, Piotr and Andrew. Sylvie too. In cafe. Am safe. Sorry. Told Anna.

Her phone stayed silent. She hoped that that was because Dad was happy with her reply, not because he was too cross to text.

'What will we do now, then?' Andrew asked.

Flora looked out. Condensation dewed the walls and rolled down the window in rivulets, blurring the colour and movement of the street. It was depressing. Andrew was right, they had to get out of here.

'Information,' Flora said.

'On Drillax?' Piotr asked.

'Let's go to mine,' Minnie said. 'We can use my dad's laptop.'

They left the cafe and bundled next door into the salon. Flora loved the grown-up smell of ammonia and alkali that permeated the salon, but it was a bit intimidating too. She had no idea what all the pots and bottles and jars were actually used for. She just brushed her hair and left it at that.

She smiled shyly at Minnie's mum, who was teasing a client's hair with a fat comb.

'We're going up to my room,' Minnie said to her mum. 'Can I use the computer, please?'

'As long as you don't bid on any auctions and buy a monster truck,' Mrs Adesina said.

'That was one time!' Andrew said indignantly.

'One time too many, Andrew,' she replied.

Piotr and Minnie sniggered as they led the way upstairs to the flat.

Minnie's room was just big enough for them all to cram in, Minnie, Andrew and Flora on the bed, Sylvie in a chair and Piotr sitting on the rug. Flora liked Minnie's room. The furniture was dark wood, solid. Her bedspread was bright orange, with snaking green shapes across it. It was cosy.

Minnie had her dad's computer open on her lap.

'Look for Drillax,' Piotr said.

Minnie typed.

'Drillax is mainly an investment bank,' Minnie said.

'Why would a bank be interested in bikes and scooters?'

Sylvie asked in confusion. 'Are you sure you've got the right company?'

Minnie shot her a deadly look. 'I'm sure. Listen.' She read from the screen. '"In a surprising recent move, Drillax announced the launch of an engineering division which will take the company in a new direction, specialising in a new form of travel – solar-powered scooters. The first product launch, the Sunblast Scooter, is expected in a matter of weeks."'

'Solar-powered scooters?' Andrew said. 'Wow! How much fun would that be? Scooters that push themselves! I wonder how fast they go. Is there a picture? When can I buy one?'

'Andrew!' Flora said, more sharply than she had intended. 'Think about it. A surprising recent move? A new direction? A first product launch? What does that tell you?'

Andrew shrugged.

'They're talking about the Breeze 5000! That's my dad's invention. That Drillax has stolen.'

'Oh.' Andrew looked contrite. 'Sorry, I forgot.'

No one quite knew what to say, so Minnie carried on reading. '"The company was established by Xander Drill, a reclusive businessperson who attended the prestigious

Northdene Prep before graduating from Oxford University." There's a picture of him. It's a bit grainy. He's got a nose like a parrot's beak!'

Andrew peered at it. 'No, I think it's just really pixelated.'

'Northdene Prep is really expensive,' Sylvie said. 'He must be loaded!'

Minnie ignored the interruption. 'Here's an article about him. It says he has refined tastes and likes the best of everything. Oh, oh, wait!'

Flora leaned closer, trying to read over Minnie's shoulder.

'"I had hoped to meet Xander Drill in his favourite restaurant",' Minnie read aloud, '"the exclusive Chos . . . Cassette . . . Chaussette d'Or, where he eats lunch every day. I hear their *moules frites* are to die for. However, Drill's PA tells me he is a very private person who insists on eating alone. He's also a creature of habit, and breaking his daily routine was impossible. So our interview was conducted over the telephone. Which is why this article is accompanied by a photograph of this reporter's cheese sandwich, rather than of Xander Drill at the Chaussette d'Or."'

'He sounds like an idiot,' Andrew said.

'He stole Dad's latest invention,' Flora said. 'Of course he's an idiot.'

Piotr laughed. 'I know. But at least he's an idiot who goes to the same restaurant every day. He's a creature of habit! We should go there, talk to the staff, see if he's done anything unusual lately. Or met anyone from Breeze.'

'What about Anna?' Flora said. 'We need to talk to her too.'

'We'll do both. First thing tomorrow, we'll go to Breeze and talk to Anna. Then, at lunchtime, we'll find the Chaussette d'Or.'

Flora smiled. They had a plan.

Chapter Seven

The following morning, Flora unpacked her suitcase. She put the folded, washing-powder-scented clothes back in their drawers. She slipped the books back on to the book-shelves. Sylvie ignored her suitcase.

Mum came in, her hair still damp from the shower. 'The childminding service just rang. They haven't anyone free.' She twisted her mobile in her hand, as though she could wring a solution from it. 'I thought I might try ringing Piotr's family or Minnie's parents. Would that be OK?'

Flora felt sorry for Mum. She didn't deserve all this extra stress. 'It's all right,' Flora said. 'We'll go to Breeze again. It was OK yesterday.' She decided not to mention the fact that they'd hardly seen Dad and they'd only stayed for a little while.

Mum nodded. 'I'll speak to your father.'

Mum stood in the hallway while she called. Flora

could hear the tinny ringing, then a weird computerised voice as it went straight to voicemail. Mum hung up without leaving a message.

'Maybe he's at work already,' Flora suggested.

Mum dialled another number. Flora heard the bright, bubbly tone of the Breeze receptionist.

'Daniel Hampshire, please,' Mum said.

Flora couldn't make out the receptionist's words, but she saw Mum's face harden into a frown. 'What about Anna, then?' she asked. 'I see. Fine. No, no message.' She hung up.

'What is it?' Flora asked.

'Your dad isn't at work today,' Mum said. 'He called in sick. Anna's not in either, also presumed sick. There's no one to look after you there. Oh, Flora.' Mum looked suddenly very tired. 'Maybe you could come to work with me? I could find a quiet corner for you both?'

'No!' Flora said quickly. Mum's law firm wasn't like law firms on the telly – there were never any car chases, or cold cases, or crime bosses. It was just contracts, contracts, contracts. Dull.

'You can't stay here.'

'I know. We'll go to Dad's and see if he's OK. He might be properly sick. We'll go and look after him.'

'All right, but if Dad's not there, or he really is poorly and you don't know what to do, call me. Are we clear?'

Flora could tell that it was killing Mum not to be in control, not to have a good plan. She nodded furiously.

'Fine. Be sensible,' Mum said.

They were sensible, Flora thought. They had backup. In the form of Piotr, Minnie and Andrew, who met them outside Dad's apartment block near the industrial estate. The block was brand new, more wood and glass than it was bricks. Dad's buzzer was the one at the top of the list. She pressed, and waited. There was no answer. She pressed again. Nothing. She glanced at Sylvie.

'Did you bring your key?' Sylvie asked.

Of course she had. Flora rummaged in her backpack, then unlocked the door. She led the way through the neat chrome-and-glass lobby, up the pale wooden steps, to his flat on the third, and top, storey. She rang the doorbell, but there was no reply. She could feel the others staring at her back, waiting for her to decide what to do. So she raised her key and unlocked the door cautiously.

The inside felt cold, as though the heating was broken. And it was dark. Was Dad really not in? Or was he too ill to get up? Flora stared at the hallway. The beige carpet and cream walls were as pale as something born under-ground. It made her shiver.

Where was Dad?

She felt worry flutter lightly in her chest. 'Dad? Dad?' The others followed her inside.

'Dad?' Flora called, louder this time.

'Hello?' The voice came from Dad's room. She held up a hand, asking the others to wait; then she moved towards the closed door. She turned the handle.

Dad's room was dark. Expensive blackout blinds were closed against the sullen day. Dad was a shape in bed, a lump under a grey duvet.

'Dad?' Flora whispered. 'Are you OK?'

'No,' Dad muttered, 'no, I'm not.'

Chapter Eight

Dad's room smelled musty, like an old book. Sylvie pushed past and twisted open the blinds. Pale winter sunlight came into the room and fell across the bed in prison bar stripes.

Dad groaned and pulled the duvet up over his head.

'Are you poorly?' Flora asked. 'Do you need a doctor? Medicine?'

'A shower?' Sylvie said pointedly.

'I'm not ill,' Dad mumbled into the cave of a bed.

Flora felt her worry turn to panic. What was the matter with Dad? He'd been fine yesterday, a bit anxious and concerned, but up and dressed and fighting.

Today it looked as though he had given up.

'Is your dad dead?' Andrew's voice came from the doorway.

'Oi! Andrew!' Dad shouted from under the duvet.

'He's not dead!' Andrew reported back to Piotr and Minnie, who were still in the hallway.

Flora pulled down the edge of the duvet, until tufts of Dad's hair were visible, then the creased skin of his forehead and his red eyes. 'What's the matter?' she asked.

'Oh, love,' Dad said.

'Work said you're ill,' Flora insisted. 'Is it serious?'

Dad pulled himself up into a sitting position. He rucked his duvet around his knees. He sighed. 'I told you I'm not ill.'

'Then what?'

Dad rubbed his face with both hands, fingertips pressed into his eyes. 'Anna's decided she wants to spend some time apart, that's all. Nothing for you to worry about. But I didn't feel like going to Breeze.'

Anna?

Flora felt something crinkle painfully inside. Anna didn't want to see Dad? And Dad didn't want to go to work? Neither of those things made sense.

She was about to speak when Sylvie stalked over and tugged at the duvet. She pulled it past Dad's pyjamas. 'Get up,' she said. 'You can't mope around. Get up and get clean and get dressed. We'll meet you in the kitchen in five minutes.'

'I don't want to,' Dad said.

'Shower!' Sylvie snapped. Then she hustled Flora and Andrew out of the room and pushed them down the hallway to the back of the flat.

In moments they heard the boiler whir into life and hot water clanked through the pipes. Dad was doing as he was told.

Flora wasn't sure how to work Dad's fancy coffee machine, so she switched on the kettle and took out a jar of instant coffee.

That's when she realised that Piotr, Minnie and Andrew were staring at the kitchen with their mouths open.

Oh.

Flora supposed it was a mouth-open type place. She'd got used to it. Dad had knocked through two rooms and replaced a wall with glass, so that the kitchen was huge and bright even on dark days. The light bounced off polished steel and white tiles and honey-coloured wood. The lines all as sleek as a sports car.

'It's like a magazine,' Minnie whispered.

Flora ladled coffee into a mug. Sylvie looked in the fridge to see if there was anything worth eating. She found some salmon and cream cheese.

'It's amazing,' Andrew said. 'I knew your dad was an engineer, but I thought he just made bikes and toys.'

Flora nodded. 'He does, but he says that he likes to make things that change the way people live.'

'It's awesome,' Piotr said.

'Thank you.' Dad's voice came from the doorway. Dad's hair was wet and curled against his forehead; his skin was red from the shower. He looked more awake, more alive. He hadn't got dressed in work clothes, just in a baggy jumper and jeans, but at least it wasn't pyjamas.

He took the mug from Flora gratefully, and sat on a breakfast stool.

Sylvie put a salmon bagel in front of him. 'Thanks,' he said. 'So, you called Breeze? Did you speak . . . to anyone?'

'Mum spoke to the receptionist,' Sylvie said. She pulled a knife and fork from a drawer and placed them next to the plate.

'Oh. So you decided to visit me?'

'We wanted to see you were all right,' Flora said.

'We were worried about your current levels of alive-ness,' Andrew added.

'Thank you, Andrew. So you all decided to come?'

'We were going to see if we could help at Breeze,' Piotr said, 'but you and . . . Anna . . . well, you weren't there.'

Dad blew on his hot coffee. 'Help? With what?'

Flora pressed her palms against a steel work surface. Was Dad seriously still trying to keep his trouble secret? 'We were there yesterday. At Breeze. It wasn't hard to work out why everyone was in a flap. We know about the Breeze 5000. We know about the spook.'

Dad's head dropped, his hand against his eyes. 'I should have known you'd want to solve the mystery. But there's nothing you can do. We have a private investigator working the case. A good one.'

'We know,' Flora said.

'I don't want you to get involved,' Dad said firmly.

'Sir,' Piotr said, 'Flora is a lot like you. She likes to know how things work, how they're put together. A mystery like this is like a sudoku puzzle, a jigsaw to work on over the school break. Especially now the twins aren't going on holiday.'

Oh. That was a low blow, Flora thought, but Dad was still listening, so she didn't object.

'We'd just like to think about the case the way you do with your inventions, that's all,' Piotr continued. 'We won't bother anyone, or get into trouble.'

Piotr had got much better at this. Flora remembered the first case they'd worked on, the theft of diamonds from the theatre. Piotr had been so tongue-tied with his first witness that he hadn't been able to ask a single sensible question. Now Dad was eating out of his hand.

'Well,' Dad said, 'I suppose it can't hurt to let you think about it. Just think, mind. No daring adventures, do you understand?'

No one said anything.

Dad took that as agreement.

'So, what do you want to know? For your puzzle?'

Piotr nodded at Flora. She pulled out her notebook and pen.

'When did the blueprints go missing?' Piotr asked.

'Over the weekend. We tested the prototype on Friday morning. I put the blueprints in the safe on Friday afternoon. Then yesterday, Monday, Drillax announced the news about their Sunblast. Janyce checked the safe; the blueprints were gone. So she called me.' Dad sighed. 'They didn't take the prototype; that stayed in the workshop. Drillax can move fast. They haven't had to pay for research, so they can sell it cheaper. We'll lose all the money we invested ... maybe worse.' Dad prodded the bagel in front of him. He hadn't taken a bite.

'Who knew the code to the safe?' Minnie asked.

'Just the partners. That's me, Janyce, Tony and Bruce.

We've been working together for ten years. It's our anniversary party on Saturday. I can't believe that any of them would betray Breeze.'

One of them must have, Flora thought. 'What did you mean,' she asked, '"maybe worse"? What's worse than losing the investment?'

Dad didn't answer right away. He looked as though he was struggling to find the right words. 'I was supposed to register the blueprints. That would mean that no other company could use the patents, could use our ideas. I was going to do it on Friday afternoon. But I was distracted. We had the holiday coming up. Anna needed to go to her parents' over the weekend, so I wasn't going to see her. I had too much to think about . . . it slipped my mind. I didn't register the blueprints. If Drillax goes ahead with their version, it's my fault. I'll be fired.'

'But it's your company!' Sylvie said.

'Perhaps not for much longer,' Dad said.

Flora couldn't believe it – one of Dad's partners had betrayed him, and it would cost him everything.

Unless they could unmask the spook.

Chapter Nine

Flora and the others watched Dad while Sylvie persuaded him to eat a little breakfast. By the time she'd finished nagging, he looked much better than he had when they'd arrived. Flora felt it was probably all right to leave him. They had to get to the Chaussette d'Or to find out what they could about Xander Drill.

Dad was on his second cup of coffee and was completing a crossword on his phone when they left. It was amazing what a stern talking-to from Sylvie could do.

Outside, even though it was late morning, the sun was still so low that even the blades of grass outside the flats cast a shadow, like a hundred tiny sundials. Flora pulled on her mittens and walked with long strides to warm up.

'Your dad looked terrible,' Andrew said cheerfully.

'And for a while there, he smelled even worse,' Minnie added.

'Well, we're going to fix it,' Flora said.

Piotr hadn't spoken for a while; then he said, 'The private investigator might get there before us. He's a grown-up, after all.'

Flora buried her hands in her pockets. 'I don't mind if he does. As long as someone saves the Breeze 5000 for Dad.' *And gets Anna to come back*, she added silently. She couldn't believe that Anna had chosen today, of all days, to stop seeing Dad. She couldn't believe that Anna could be that cruel.

The Chaussette d'Or was on the fringes of town, at the point where the streets of solid terraced houses gave way to shopfronts and roundabouts. The restaurant was set back from the road. It had once been a substantial town house, but now the front garden had been land-scaped to provide parking; the drive was dotted with low lights; a sign was positioned beside the gates – a golden sock on a blue background. The heavy black door was closed, though the place didn't look shut – more unwelcoming.

'I don't think they are going to let us in,' Minnie said.

The five of them stood on the paved drive.

'I wonder if there's a back door?' Andrew said. 'I bet there's a back door. We should look.' He marched towards the side of the building, ignoring the imposing main entrance.

They all sighed in relief. No one wanted to get thrown out of a fancy restaurant before they were old enough to eat in one.

As they walked around the yew hedge that shrouded the garden, Andrew muttered to himself. 'Fancy restaurants should serve fish finger sandwiches. There's nothing wrong with fish finger sandwiches. I don't know why people would want to eat anything else. It's the best meal there is.'

The back of the house looked less intimidating. Here, three big metal bins backed on to a metal fire escape. A couple of rickety chairs stood around an upturned plastic crate – an impromptu, outdoor staffroom. A girl sat in one of the chairs, cradling a mug, her feet on the crate. She was wrapped in a heavy, puffy coat but had taken her shoes off, despite the cold, and was flexing her toes back and forth.

'Hello,' Piotr said.

'Hello,' she replied in a Polish accent.

Piotr grinned. His Polish, thanks to his parents, was perfect. He said something to the girl that Flora didn't understand.

The girl giggled. She replied in a bubbling stream of words that sounded delighted as sunrise.

She and Piotr spoke quickly for a few minutes, then he flipped back into English. 'This is Kamila,' he said, 'she's a waitress here. She has a ten-minute break before the lunch rush. Kamila, these are my friends Minnie, Andrew, Flora and Sylvie.'

Kamila smiled warmly at them. 'Piotr explains to me that you are investigators. You look for information. Like tiny, secret police.' She giggled again. 'It would be pleasure to help you. I like tiny, secret police children. Not like the horrible, rude investigator who was here earlier.'

'An investigator came?' Flora said. 'Did he ask about Xander Drill?'

Kamila nodded.

Oh. Flora was part pleased that the PI had started on the case. That was good, she told herself. But another unexpected part of her wished that she could be the one to help Dad.

'He was rude man,' Kamila said, wide-eyed, 'like Mr Drill. They are peas in peas' pods. Both demanding things, never saying thank you. It does not hurt to be polite, no?'

Piotr spoke again in Polish.

Kamila gave him a delighted look. 'You are nice boy. Sit!'

61

She waved at the plastic chairs. There wasn't room for all of them, so Andrew sat on the plastic crate. Kamila sighed as she lifted her feet off the crate. 'Waitressing is too many blisters. I should have been beautician,' she said sadly. 'So, you want to know about Mr Drill? He is here every day, like he is a clock.'

'Have you ever seen him with anyone?' Minnie asked.

Flora pulled out her phone and brought up the Breeze website. There were smiling photos of the partners. 'Did you ever see him with any of these people?'

She showed the screen to Kamila.

Kamila shook her head. 'I do not think so. He is here with a security guard between twelve thirty and one fifteen every day. He speaks to no one, except to complain: *This food is too cold; this food is too spicy; this food is too orange.* Pah.'

Flora wondered what food could be too orange.

'He smiles at no one,' Kamila continued, 'he looks at no one.'

'He eats alone?'

'Yes. Always. No friends.'

'He sounds lovely,' Flora said.

Kamila looked at her in confusion. 'Am I not just saying he is pig?'

'Yes. Sorry. Sarcasm,' Flora stuttered.

Kamila scowled. Piotr said something soothing in Polish. Kamila tutted, then said, 'I have only once seen him with anyone else.'

'Who?' Piotr asked. He pointed at the phone. 'One of these people?'

Kamila shrugged. 'I told the private investigator, I don't know. I was late for work last Sunday. I slept through my alarm. Until nearly lunchtime! I run to get here. I pass Mr Drill's car, in the car park here. Someone stands at the window, passing something inside. I don't know what, an envelope, maybe. It's strange, to meet in a car park, I think, but then I remember my boss and I run faster.'

Flora felt her eagerness turn to disappointment.

Kamila had seen the spook, but hadn't bothered to look at them! 'Was it a man or a woman, do you think? Young? Old? What were they wearing?' Flora asked.

Kamila shrugged. 'This country, it does not know winter. This is not cold. But still, people dress like Arctic. The person I saw was same – big coat, scarf, hat, gloves. Wrapped up like mummy.'

Kamila pushed her feet into her polished black shoes. 'I must get back to work.' She patted her sleek hair down, though there wasn't a wisp out of place.

'Thank you for helping us,' Flora said. 'Is there any other detail you can remember? Anything at all?'

Kamila looked thoughtful. 'I have been thinking about this since this morning. I have remembered one thing. I was going to call the investigator, to tell him. But he was so rude, I don't know if I will.'

'What is it?' Flora asked.

'The person I saw, all wrapped up, I remember they held the envelope in their left hand. I think the person I saw is left-handed. I notice because I was left-handed, but my school was very strict. They made me write with my right hand. It was hard. Left-handed people in this country are very lucky. I remember thinking – that is a lucky person. Does that help?'

'Yes,' Flora said, 'that helps a lot.'

Chapter Ten

Kamila scooped up her empty mug and headed towards the back door.

'Wait!' Andrew called to her. 'Do you think we could speak to Xander? What time will he be here?'

She shook her head. 'I do not recommend that you try. He has security staff who will throw you out on the hard ground if you even stand too close.'

Flora thought that it was very unlikely that Xander Drill would tell them who the spook was anyway. There was no point getting hurt for nothing. 'Thank you, Kamila, you've been really kind.'

'Will I tell the private investigator?' Kamila asked, rolling the final 'r' like mouthwash on her tongue. 'That I remembered the person who spoke to Mr Drill was a left-handed person? I do not think I should. He was very rude.'

Piotr shook his head. 'Don't worry, we'll tell him.'

Flora felt a pinching disappointment. But she had to admit to herself that Piotr was right. There was an expert on the case now; they should share all the information they had. It wasn't about solving the mystery, it was about doing what was best for Dad.

They waved Kamila goodbye and retraced their steps back to the street.

'What now?' Minnie asked.

'Well, I think we need to pass on what we've learned from Kamila to the PI,' Piotr said.

'And then find out which of the partners is left-handed,' Flora added.

Sylvie, who hadn't said a word for a long time, suddenly spoke. 'I can't believe Anna dumped Dad. What is wrong with her? How could she do that to him?'

Her mind was obviously not on left-handed spooks, or rude private investigators. Flora slipped her arm through her twin's and gave Sylvie a small squeeze.

'It just doesn't seem fair, you know?' Sylvie said softly.

There was nothing Flora could say. It wasn't fair.

They headed towards Breeze together, under a grey, bin-liner sky. They would deliver the information to the PI and decide what to do from there.

At Breeze, the receptionist gave them a hurried smile. 'Back again?' she said. 'Your dad isn't in today.'

'We know,' Sylvie said. 'We were wondering if the private investigator is here? We have something to tell him.'

The receptionist frowned and looked at the scraps of paper on her desk, notes and missed calls and records of numbers. 'Here it is!' she said, and pulled out a card. 'Wendell Shtick. I'll call.' She dialled quickly, and waited. 'Mr Shtick? The young Hampshire girls are at reception for you. With friends. No, reception. Reception. Oh, all right. Yes.' She hung up.

She looked a little taken aback. 'He says he's too busy.'

'He won't see us?' Piotr asked in astonishment. 'But we have something very important to share that he'll want to know.'

'Well, he says no. He's a very . . . terse person.' The receptionist grinned conspiratorially. 'Perhaps he needs to be shaken up a bit. He's in your dad's office.' She pressed the buzzer that opened the door into the offices. 'You know the way?'

She gave Flora a broad wink as she and the others headed inside.

It was a short stomp to Dad's office. When Sylvie

pushed open the door, Flora caught her first glimpse of Private Investigator Wendell Shtick.

He was kneeling on the floor in front of a closed safe. He wore a thick dark coat and a navy woollen scarf, even though he was indoors. His black hair was swept off his face with solid-fix concrete gel. His dark beard was trimmed close to his chin. He looked much more stylish than she'd imagined.

He scowled in the general direction of the doorway. The pen he was holding paused over his notepad. 'What?' he said. 'Did that imbecile of a receptionist not understand my instructions? I am busy and I have no interest in hearing the prattling of children.'

Wow.

Flora was taken aback. It wasn't often that she was made to feel small and silly. Most of the time, she forgot that she even was a child! It was only when people's elbows accidentally hit her on the head that she was reminded that she was still quite small. But Wendell Shtick made her feel about five years old.

'We have some information,' Piotr said. 'It might help you.'

'The day I need help from schoolchildren will be the day I hang up my PI badge for good,' Wendell said. 'I've heard about you and your meddling. You solve one crime –'

'Two, actually,' Andrew interrupted. 'We've solved two crimes.'

Shtick glared at him. 'You solve two crimes, and suddenly you're a Poirot–Sherlock mash-up? You think you're Poirlock? Well, I've solved literally half a dozen crimes. Maybe more.'

'How do you know about us?' Piotr asked.

Shtick turned back to examine the safe once more. Flora thought he wasn't going to answer. Then he said, 'I have my sources. This isn't the first time I've helped Breeze. I nearly won a case for one of the partners. Your names were mentioned. In passing. No one was impressed or anything.'

Flora noticed Andrew stand a little prouder. 'We stopped illegal smuggling of precious works of art. And found a stolen necklace for a film star.'

'Humph. I heard you'd have been in trouble if the police hadn't stepped in. I heard it was a police officer who turned up just in time to save you. Well, I'm not having you getting into danger and leaving me to fill out the insurance paperwork. Go on, clear out of it.'

'It wasn't like that!' Andrew said angrily.

Minnie placed her hands on her hips. 'You don't know what you're talking about!'

Wendell rose slowly to his feet. His long coat flapped down to his knees. He put his notepad and pen into his left pocket and turned to face them. 'I do not need your help,' he said firmly. 'This is an open and shut case. The slowest of fools could solve it in a heartbeat.'

'You've solved it?' Flora asked in amazement. They'd only just got started! How had Wendell unmasked the spook before they had even got close?

'Of course. A valuable secret goes missing. The boss's girlfriend disappears the same day. Two and two make four.'

'Anna?' Flora felt her chest tighten. Wendell suspected Anna of stealing from Breeze? No way. She'd never betray Dad. She'd stood by him through long weekends of work, through Sylvie's strops when they'd first got together, through all kinds of worries.

She's not with him today, though.

Flora pushed the unwelcome thought right out of her head. Anna was great. She and Dad would work out their problems. That was all there was to it.

'What's your evidence?' Piotr asked.

'As if I'd share any of it with you!' Wendell said scornfully.

Flora tugged Piotr's elbow. The warmth of his woollen jumper felt comforting. 'Come on,' she said quietly, 'we're doing no good here.'

Piotr gave Wendell Shtick a look of disgust. But he nodded and turned to lead them out of Dad's office.

'You lot stay out of this, is that clear?' Wendell yelled as they left.

Sylvie was the last out. She grabbed the door handle with both hands and gave it a very satisfying slam behind her.

'Now what?' Minnie said. 'Do you believe him?'

Flora shook her head. 'It can't have been Anna. She wouldn't do that to Dad, not for anything. And she doesn't know the code to the safe.'

'Dad might have told her,' Sylvie said. 'He trusts her.'

'And so do I,' Flora replied.

Sylvie was quiet. For the time being.

'If the stupid private investigator isn't interested in the clues,' Andrew said, 'then we'll have to investigate them for him. We know that Xander met with a left-handed person, and he was all secretive about it. The timeline works too. Your dad said the blueprints went into the safe last Friday, then this left-handed person met Xander Drill on Sunday. There's plenty of time for someone to have accessed the safe between those times. It fits perfectly. What we have to do is find out if any of the people who know the combination to the safe are also left-handed.'

'How are we going to do that?' Flora asked.

'Elementary, my dear Poirlock. We investigate,' Andrew said with a flourish. Then he pulled tongues at the closed door and the rude man behind it.

Chapter Eleven

Flora put her backpack down on the grey floor tiles of the corridor. She rifled through and took out her notebook. With her sparkly gel pen, she made quick notes about that morning's discoveries. 'There are four people who know the access code to the safe –' she glanced at Sylvie '– and none of them are Anna. Dad is one. The other partners make up the rest – Janyce, Tony and Bruce.'

'So we need to find out which of them is left-handed. And whether they have any motive for leaking the blueprints,' Piotr said.

Flora nodded and put the notebook away. The corridor was empty. They could hear the clatter of fingers on keyboards, the swoosh of a photocopier somewhere in the distance, but for the time being, they were alone.

'No time like the present,' Andrew said. 'We're inside

the offices. We should find out right now. Let's split up, cover more ground.'

'I'm going to talk to Janyce, and I don't mind being on my own,' Sylvie said quickly.

Flora was surprised. Usually Sylvie hated being left out – last time they'd investigated a mystery Sylvie had gone off in a strop after Minnie made her work alone. Why on earth had she volunteered now?

Flora didn't have time to wonder. Andrew linked arms with her and winked. 'Me and Flora will take Tony,' he said.

'Fine,' Piotr agreed. 'That leaves me and Minnie to find Bruce. Where will he be, do you think?'

'In engineering, past the atrium.'

'So, what's an atrium?' Minnie asked Flora. 'How will we know when we're past it?'

'It's the big glass room at the bottom of the staircase,' Flora explained. 'Like a giant greenhouse. You can't miss it. The workshop is through the doors at the far end. Meet back here in half an hour and we'll see what we've learned.'

Left-handedness should be simple to find out. Motive? Harder, but still possible. Flora hoped that they would soon be telling Dad which member of the team was the traitor.

Chapter Twelve

Piotr and Minnie headed off together. Flora was quite right – *As usual*, Piotr thought. It was impossible to miss the atrium. Like some kind of futuristic school hall, it connected the two halves of the building. A few people milled about there, sitting on pale wooden benches, under architectural plants – all green angles and brown curves. No one stopped the children though, or asked what they were doing.

No wonder stuff got stolen.

They pushed open the blue doors on the far side of the atrium. They were in a long, narrow corridor. There were no doors along the grey walls, just the occasional window. No carpet on the floor either, only bare concrete. Piotr realised that the corridor was more of a covered walkway, to get from the plush offices to the noisy workroom beyond. He knew it would be noisy because he could already faintly hear the thudding of machinery, even though the walkway was maybe a hundred metres long.

'Come on, let's find him,' Piotr said, setting off. As they got closer to the double doors at the end, the noise got louder. He heard the whine of gear belts, the *slam*, *bash*, *smash* of metal hitting metal.

There were windows set into the doors, above the handles. Minnie could see inside. Piotr had to go on tiptoes.

They were looking in at a small lobby, with the workshop beyond. The lobby was a bit grimy and dark, like a bus shelter tacked on to the doorway. Beyond its dusty glass walls they could see the huge workshop, full of big pieces of machinery, grinding, cutting, crunching metal parts. A few people stood keenly watching the processes from behind safety goggles.

Were any of the goggle-wearers Bruce? As well as the goggles, most of them had ear defenders and white coats too. It was impossible to tell whether the people were men or women, old or young, white or black; they were just walking protective equipment from head to toe.

Minnie pushed open the door.

Even in the lobby, they could feel the heat generated by the machines, and smell the tangy acid of oil and metal dust. It was nothing like the clean corporate design of the office space. A few white coats hung on hooks. Minnie lifted two down and handed one to Piotr before slipping on her own. His was a bit big, with the sleeves falling below his wrists, but a big disguise was better than no disguise at all.

'Should we go in?' Piotr asked Minnie.

'What?'

'Should we go in?'

'I can't hear you!'

'Never mind.'

'What?'

Piotr shook his head and grabbed the handle to the door that divided the lobby from the workroom.

Now the noise really was deafening.

There was no way that they were going to be able to interview anyone here. They'd have to write their questions on signs and hold them up.

But at least the noise meant that no one so much as looked their way when they came in.

Piotr scanned the room. He counted eight people, all in white coats. Did any of them look Bruce-like? Or give off Bruce-ish vibes? Not really.

Then Minnie gave him a small nudge. She nodded towards a door. It was painted the same mushroom grey as the walls, so blended right in. Except for the black print on a plaque:

Bruce Harvey
Head of Engineering

They skirted around the industrious staff and the industrial machines until they reached the door. A few people glanced in their direction, but no one tried to stop them. It was amazing what a white coat could do. Piotr tapped lightly on the grey door, then realised that no one would hear that tap with all the thumping going on, so he gave it a really hard knock.

He thought he heard a reply.

He opened the door.

The space beyond must have once been an office. It had shelves with files, a desk, a phone. But over time, it had evolved into a mini-workshop, as though it was being absorbed into the bigger room beyond. In the centre was a huge workbench, its scorched and scarred top evidence of the years of use it had had. All kinds of objects were scattered across the bench's surface – motors, wheels, spokes, circuit boards and casings, jars of oils and liquids. Piotr noticed that the office had no windows. The bright light came from a circle of bulbs hung on a movable arm on the ceiling, like a lamp in an operating theatre.

The floor was littered too – short sections of wire that made Piotr think of the hair clippings in Minnie's mum's salon; crumpled sheets of paper, some nearer the bin than others; discarded tools; dead bike parts: it looked like the shoreline at a turning tide.

It was a mess.

The man who stood in the middle of it all wasn't much better. He was tall and skinny, with his shirt flaps untucked from his trousers. His tie was stained with blobs of custard that dripped right over the school motto. His trousers had smears of black oil on the thighs, as though there had been nothing better for the man to wipe mucky fingers on.

He looked over at them and blinked a few times.

Minnie closed the door behind them; immediately the noise was muffled.

The man blinked again. 'Work experience?' he said in a tremulous voice.

'No,' Piotr said.

'Bruce?' Minnie asked. 'Bruce Harvey?'

'The same,' the man said. He picked up a twist of metal from the workbench in his *left* hand and turned it up towards the light. Piotr felt a leap of excitement. Then

Bruce passed it from his left hand to his right hand and examined it again.

Hmm.

'We were hoping you might have time to talk,' Piotr said.

'Talk?' Bruce said the word as though he were only slightly acquainted with the idea. 'About what?'

Piotr and Minnie shared a glance. Both realised they had failed to work out a cover story.

'A school project . . .' Minnie said.

'An article for the junior paper . . .' Piotr said, at exactly the same time.

'Well,' Bruce looked confused, 'which is it?'

Piotr sighed. He had thought he was getting better at this. There was nothing for it but the truth. 'We're friends of Flora and Sylvie,' he began.

'The Hampshire twins?'

'You know them?' Minnie asked.

'Of course. Well, I know *of* them. Their father is very proud of them. Almost as proud of them as he is of the Tour de France bike. Have you seen it? It's in reception. It is truly wonderful.' He held up the object to the light. 'I wondered if we could use a new alloy in this gear mechanism. Does this feel light to you?'

He passed the silver shape to Piotr and looked at it quizzically.

Piotr weighed the metal in his palm. 'It's very light,' he said, and passed it back.

Bruce seemed to have forgotten that he had no idea who Piotr and Minnie were.

Piotr decided to stop worrying about their lack of cover story.

'Did you help make that bike?' Minnie asked.

Bruce nodded. 'I played my small part, yes. Nothing is made by Breeze that I haven't tried and tested myself.'

'Including the Breeze 5000?'

'What do you know about that?' Bruce asked, his voice suddenly sharp.

'It's a solar-powered scooter. Its blueprints have been stolen. That's all we know,' Piotr said. 'But it sounds amazing. I'd love to have a go on one some day.'

Bruce's attention turned back to the alloy. 'Oh, it is tremendous fun. They go much faster than you'd think. Entirely on the sun's energy. Racing our two prototypes was the most fun Daniel and I have had in ages. He won, but I came a close second! I haven't laughed that much since my third wife fell off an elephant in Bali.'

Piotr looked at Minnie. Would someone who seemed to like Mr Hampshire so much really betray him?

'Do you have any idea how the blueprints might have been leaked?' Piotr asked.

Bruce shook his head forcefully. 'No, not at all. Security here is very tight. Nothing leaves the building. There are no windows in the engineering spaces, so no one can see inside. All the computers are password protected. There's even a mobile phone jammer installed in the engineering wing to stop people making calls or taking photographs. It's impossible to spy on Breeze!'

'Until now,' Piotr said.

Bruce hung his head sadly. 'Yes. It's terrible.'

Minnie pulled out a pen. 'I wonder,' she said, 'whether you might give me your autograph. I'd love to be able to tell people I met the person who invented a Tour de France-winning bike.'

Piotr tried not to smile.

Bruce raised his head. Piotr noticed that he had gone bright red, and looked as pleased as if Minnie had offered him a Nobel Prize. 'Well,' he said, 'I didn't do it single-handed.'

'Please?' Minnie said sweetly.

Bruce chuckled again. Then he tore a sheet of paper

from a pad on his desk and took the pen from Minnie. With his right hand. He drew his signature with a dramatic flourish.

He handed it back to Minnie with a smile.

Piotr felt satisfied. Bruce liked his job, and he was right-handed. 'Thank you for seeing us, sir,' Piotr said. 'I do hope we didn't disturb you.'

'Not at all. Young minds are to be encouraged, I always say. Unless they're breaking something.' Bruce bent down over the workbench and leaned in so close to examine a spring that Piotr worried it would get tangled in his eyebrows.

'Thank you!' Minnie said, waving her autograph. Bruce didn't reply. They backed out of the office, through the cacophony of the workroom, and back into the long corridor that led to the atrium.

When the double doors closed behind them, Minnie grinned. 'One suspect eliminated!' she said. 'I wonder how the others are getting on?'

Chapter Thirteen

'What's Tony like?' Andrew asked.

Flora and Andrew had watched the others go to find their targets. Now the two of them were walking towards reception, keeping an eye out for Dad's business partner. But all they saw was harassed-looking people typing rapidly and answering shrill telephones.

'He's all right, I suppose,' Flora said.

'That's the nastiest thing I've ever heard you say about anyone,' Andrew said.

Flora laughed. That was probably true. 'Well,' she said. 'He's a bit slimy. He and Dad were friends at university. Tony went into banking and made loads of money. When Dad and Bruce had the idea for the first Breeze bike, he went to Tony to ask him to invest. Tony loved the idea.'

'So what's the problem?' Andrew asked.

'He just, well, he pretends everyone is his best friend,

even when they definitely aren't. And he's the sort of person who wears sunglasses indoors. You'll see.'

They peeped into offices, looking through the panes of glass in the doors at the staff. Flora didn't spot Tony. Was he there today? He didn't work every day, she knew that. He liked to drive around in his sports car with the roof down, even in winter. He did that for hours sometimes. Even though he owned a bike factory.

She was about to give up and go back to the start to retrace their steps when she heard Tony's laugh. It was a sound Flora had heard many, many times – loud, booming, and somehow not quite real, as though Tony had learned to laugh from watching other people.

He was in the staffroom.

He sat with two other people at a table in the otherwise deserted area. The space was light and airy, with huge skylights set in the roof to let the sunshine in. There was a mini kitchen at one end of the room, with the sort of fancy coffee machine that Dad liked. The tables were long, pale wood, with simple, elegant chairs set around them. Each table was clean and brightly polished.

Flora didn't recognise the two women who sat with Tony, but they smiled warmly at his joke. He was making himself crease with laughter.

Then he noticed her and Andrew. 'Sylvie! Or is it Flora-dora?' he boomed, using an old – stupid – nickname.

Andrew snorted.

'Shut it,' she hissed at him. 'It's Flora,' she said, louder.

'Sorry, ladies,' Tony said to the two women at his table, 'it seems a young damsel in distress wants me.'

They stood up and beamed, before heading back to the admin offices.

'Pull up a pew, Flora-dora, and introduce me to your young knight in shining velour.'

'Slimy,' Andrew whispered.

Yup. No question.

She sat down opposite him. Andrew sat beside her. 'Tony, this is Andrew. Andrew, this is Tony.'

'You look *très* serious,' Tony said in a mock French accent.

'It is serious around here at the moment,' Flora said gravely.

'I know! I thought owning a company would be fun, but it's more depressing than an *EastEnders* omnibus,' Tony complained. 'Your dad hasn't had a day off in months. What's the point of having money if you never have time to spend it?'

Flora laid her palms flat on the table and leaned towards Tony. 'So, you don't think my dad should be here?'

'Of course I don't! He should be in Tenerife, with you guys. And his girlfriend. Instead he's here, trying to fix the world.'

'Do you think you should be in charge instead?' Flora asked. Shadows flitted around the room as birds flew over the skylights.

'Me?' Tony laughed. 'No. I love the company, but I don't want to be here any more than I can help. This is my pension, my nest egg. My way to retire to the South of France and eat croissants all day.'

'Who do you think would have sabotaged the company?' Andrew asked. 'If you had to accuse someone?'

'How am I to know? I'm hardly here. I'm a silent partner.' Tony laughed loudly. 'Well, silent in one sense of the word. I never comment on how your father runs the company as long as I see a profit. Now that that profit is under threat I might be here more often. The board will want that, I imagine.'

'The board?' Flora asked, imagining something to do with chopping vegetables.

'The management board,' Tony explained. 'They run the place.'

'I thought my dad ran it?'

'Only because management let him. No, in all this mess your dad is going to need to keep the board on side. And Janyce is power-hungry. She'll be angling for them to give her full control, I'm sure.'

Andrew leaned in closer too. 'What do you think of Xander Drill?'

'The man is a viperous weasel in a Versace suit.'

'Don't you like suits?' Andrew said. Tony was wearing jeans and a polo shirt. As Flora had predicted, there was an iridescent pair of sunglasses balanced on the top of his head. In February.

'No,' Tony laughed. 'Suits are for people who don't know how to dress.'

'I like your sunglasses,' Andrew said. 'Designer? They're proper entrepreneur's shades. I'm going to have a pair like that when I grow up.'

Flora rolled her eyes. What had Tony's stupid sunglasses to do with anything?

Andrew was leaning halfway over the table now, close enough to whisper. 'What kind of car do you drive? Is it fast?'

Tony chuckled. 'A Porsche Cayman.'

Flora tutted. If Andrew was any shallower he'd be two-dimensional.

'Flora,' Andrew said, 'give me a pen and a piece of paper.'

She could have squealed at him. But she couldn't stop herself from being polite, so she handed over a pen and her precious notebook.

Andrew laboured over the page. Then he held it up. *Portch Keeman*, he'd written.

Tony smirked again. 'No, son, not like that. Hand me the pen.'

Andrew did as Tony said.

Tony took it with his right hand.

Then smoothly passed it to his left.

He took the pad, crossed out Andrew's attempt and neatly spelled out the make and model. With his left hand.

'Every entrepreneur needs to know how to spell Porsche,' he said with a wink.

Chapter Fourteen

Sylvie decided that the others could search for left-handed spooks all they liked.

She had another target in mind.

She'd agreed to go and interview Janyce Penning for one reason, and it had nothing to do with missing blueprints.

Janyce was Anna's boss.

If anyone knew whether Anna was trustworthy, or the sort of terrible person who would date Dad and wheedle information out of him before throwing him aside and trampling on his heart like some kind of Turkish delight-wielding ice queen, that person would be Janyce.

Sylvie headed towards the communications team office.

Anna had taken them there just the day before. It felt like forever ago.

There was no one in the room. Anna's desk was abandoned, the computer switched off, papers and pens arranged neatly, undisturbed. Janyce had an anteroom off the main office, built with glass walls so that she could keep an eye on her staff. Two other desks were arranged between Anna's and Janyce's. Sylvie wondered where everyone was. Then she realised that the more time she spent wondering, the less quality time she'd have for snooping.

She crossed the room and switched on Anna's computer, casting an eye over her desk as the computer whirred into life. There was that photo of Dad. Yuck. Though the one of Mr Tumnus, the cat, was cute.

The computer chirruped as the black screen turned blue. Then a white rectangle appeared.

Password.

Rats.

Sylvie could have kicked the desk. Her one perfect opportunity to sneak a look at what Dad's girlfriend – ex-girlfriend, she corrected herself – did all day, and she'd failed at the first attempt.

Unless Anna was as rubbish at inventing a password as everyone else in the world.

Sylvie quickly typed <u>MrTumnus</u>.

Not accepted.

She pulled open the top drawer of the desk. Maybe Anna was daft enough to write her password on a Post-it note? The drawer had a brown folder in it, with a stupid smiley face drawn on it. She lifted the flap, but it just held some old photos. No password.

She looked wildly at the desk. The photo: a framed shot of Anna and Dad on a beach somewhere, both of them smiling like idiots, too close to the camera. Sylvie's nose crinkled. At least they weren't kissing.

She typed again. *Daniel.* Dad's first name.

The computer chirruped again and the desktop icons appeared.

Interesting.

Anna had chosen Dad as her password. That had to mean something. Did she care about him after all? Or was it all part of a plan to get to the company secrets?

Sylvie opened the email program. The inbox was full of unread emails, all with boring-sounding subjects like 'Meeting Minutes – Tuesday' and 'Company History Presentation Query'. She closed it. There was nothing there. She opened the web browser and clicked 'History'. She could learn where Anna had been online. Perhaps there was something suspicious in her internet browsing.

Hmm. That was odd.

Yesterday afternoon, Anna had clicked on hotel websites. Sylvie opened the links. One site appeared more than once, as though she'd been checking it against the others. A hotel in the town centre. The Ash Tree.

Why on earth was Anna looking for a hotel in her own hometown? It didn't make any sense.

Unless she was looking for somewhere to hide. Somewhere to lie low until the fuss blew over and she could start a new life with Xander Drill's dirty money?

Sylvie felt a thrill rush through her. She had never liked Anna, not ever, not even when she'd taken them on a department store trip and bought them loads of presents. It had been Dad's money she'd been spending anyway.

Anna was no good for them. And she, Sylvie, had found the proof.

'What exactly are you doing?' An imperious voice interrupted Sylvie's reading. She clicked the browser screen closed with a fumble. In the doorway, Janyce Penning stood, glaring.

'I was just looking for a game or something. While I wait for Anna.'

'This is a place of work, not a playground. I thought I'd made that clear to Daniel yesterday,' Janyce snapped.

She still looked immaculate, despite all the drama. She was tall and thin, with greying hair cut in a sharp bob. Her shoes were bright red. She walked into the room as though she were leading a marching band.

Wendell Shtick followed behind.

Sylvie switched off the computer completely.

He stopped dead at the sight of her. 'You again?'

Sylvie shrugged. 'I get around.'

'And you say that's Anna's desk?' he gasped. 'Get away from it this second! You might be disturbing crucial evidence.'

Yes, Sylvie thought, *crucial evidence that Dad's ex-girlfriend is a witch*. Still, she stood up and stepped away from the desk.

Wendell shook his head. 'I don't like this. I don't like this at all. Unsupervised children should not be allowed on-site after such a sensitive security breach. It's not reasonable. It's not welcome. It's not . . .'

'Hygienic?' Janyce suggested with a sniff. 'I entirely agree, Mr Shtick. I shall make arrangements with reception to put a stop to it immediately. Children are so very sticky,' Janyce said, as an afterthought.

'I'm not sticky!' Sylvie said hotly. 'I'm quite meticulously clean; my dance instructor always says so.'

'Then maybe you should return to your dance instructor?' Janyce said firmly, 'Instead of cluttering up my office in a time of crisis.'

The word *crisis* reminded Sylvie that she had another task to fulfil, the one that the others were expecting her to do: find out whether Janyce had a motive for ruining the company, and find out whether she was left-handed.

Sylvie had no idea how to subtly, sneakily, cunningly get information from Janyce without her noticing. So she decided to come right out with it instead.

'Did you give the blueprints to Xander Drill?' Sylvie said.

Janyce gasped. Her hands flew to cover her heart, as though the shock might make it beat right out of her chest. 'Me? What a question! How dare you! I've built up this company from nothing. Me! Daniel and Bruce are obsessed with inventing. Tony only cares about his investment. Actually keeping this place up and running has been my life's work! Every sale has been down to me and my team. I've never been so insulted!'

Wendell pulled a wheeled chair closer and helped the hyperventilating Janyce into it. 'Call yourself an investigator?' he drawled. 'That was the worst line of enquiry I've ever had the misfortune to witness.'

Sylvie shrugged. Unless Janyce was a really, really good actress, then she looked innocent enough. So as far as Sylvie could see, she'd done a good job of investigating. There was just one more thing to test. Sylvie stood and marched over to the water cooler. She tugged at the dispenser of blue cups and filled one. She handed it to Janyce.

Who took it with her *right* hand.

Sylvie considered her job done.

Janyce was innocent, and Anna was looking more and more guilty. She gave Wendell a cheery grin and left the room.

Chapter Fifteen

Flora and Andrew sat waiting impatiently in the corridor behind reception. Everyone was supposed to meet back there after speaking to their suspect. But there was no sign of the others. Flora hoped none of them had got into any trouble.

Flora worried at the brown weave of the chair, picking at its tightly spun wool. That was what investigating was like, she thought, pulling at one loose thread until the whole thing unravelled.

'They're back!' Andrew said, jumping up.

Minnie and Piotr marched up the corridor towards them. Sylvie stalked behind, her arms folded like a shield in front of her.

'I can't believe they're chucking me out of Dad's own company!' Sylvie said, by way of hello.

'Chucking you out?' Flora asked anxiously, checking

the corridor behind Sylvie. Sure enough, Wendell Shtick followed, like a police escort. He was silent, but his steely look and pinched mouth meant only one thing – get out. Flora and Andrew fell into step with the rest of the chagrined parade, through the door, back into reception.

Once they were outside, Wendell spoke to the receptionist. 'These children are not to be allowed back into Breeze without suitable adult supervision. Is that clear?'

The receptionist nodded mutely.

The gang found themselves out on the street.

'Sylvie,' Minnie said, 'what did you do to upset him?'

'Oh, right, so this is my fault now?' Sylvie flared.

'I. Don't. Know. *That's* why I'm asking,' Minnie replied.

'Hey,' Piotr said, 'there's no need to fight. Come on, let's go back to Marsh Road and share what we've found out.'

Minnie and Sylvie ignored each other, faces turned away, all the way back to the cafe.

Eileen brought a tray of drinks over, as the cafe was quiet. Flora pulled out her notebook.

'Right,' she said. 'Left-handed suspects. And motives for ruining Breeze. Go.'

'Bruce is right-handed,' Minnie said.

Flora scribbled quickly.

'I can't remember whether Anna is right-handed or not,' Sylvie said. 'Can you, Flora?'

'Sylvie!' Flora snapped. 'Anna isn't a suspect. She wouldn't hurt Dad, you know that.'

'Yes, because he looked so happy earlier.' Sylvie's pale lips curled into a smirk.

'She's right-handed, anyway,' Flora said crossly. 'I can't believe in all the months you've known her you haven't noticed.'

'How about motives?' Piotr asked, clumsily changing the subject.

They looked at each other across the tray of fizzing drinks and tangled straws. Which of the people with access to the safe wanted the business to fail? And why?

'I can't believe that any of them want to ruin Breeze,' Flora said softly. 'Why would they? They've built it up from scratch.'

'Janyce said that Tony only cares about money,' Sylvie said. 'Perhaps he thought they weren't making enough and that selling ideas to Drillax would be more profitable?'

Flora wrote that down.

'And Tony is left-handed!' Piotr said, tapping the tabletop in excitement. 'He could be our prime suspect!'

'Well,' Andrew replied, 'Tony said that Janyce was only interested in power. Maybe she set your dad up to get fired. She stabbed him in the back!' He plunged his straw into his drink so hard that it popped straight back out again and splattered dark droplets on the tabletop.

'Janyce is right-handed,' Sylvie said. 'And furious that this has happened.'

Flora added that to her notes. 'So Tony is our main suspect? This is fantastic stuff, guys. Would he make more money from selling the plans to Xander than he does from Breeze? If he would then we've got a motive too.'

'Who would know?' Piotr asked. 'I mean, we can't get back into the building now –'

'Thanks to Sylvie,' Minnie interrupted.

'We were all snooping,' Piotr said, trying to throw oil on some very choppy waters. 'We all got ourselves barred. So we can't go and ask the people who work there.'

'We could ask my dad,' Flora suggested.

'We could ask Anna,' Sylvie countered quickly. 'We can try to get the truth out of her.'

Flora felt a flurry of excitement. Yes, Anna would

know all the gossip about the partners. She'd know if Tony wasn't to be trusted.

'We'll go to her flat.'

Sylvie made a sniffing sound.

'What?' Flora asked.

'Shows how much you know about precious Anna.'

'What's that supposed to mean?' Minnie asked.

'Nothing!' Sylvie held up her hands in surrender. 'Nothing at all. Yes, let's go and visit Anna at her flat and see what she has to say. Just don't be surprised if Anna isn't quite as innocent she pretends to be, that's all.'

Neither of the twins had been inside Anna's flat before, but they had waited outside in the car while Dad dropped her off after days out, so they knew how to get there. It was about ten minutes' walk from the cafe, past the block of flats where Andrew lived with his mum.

On the way, Flora and Piotr walked at the back of the group. Flora liked to talk things over with Piotr. He wasn't excitable like Andrew, or prickly like Minnie and Sylvie could be. He was always kind.

'Is your dad doing OK?' he asked.

'I don't know. I'll call him later to see. Breeze means the whole world to him.' Flora imagined Dad, alone at home, brooding over the lost blueprints. He wouldn't be able to cope with being forced to leave Breeze too.

'We'll help him, I know we will,' Piotr said.

Flora tried to smile. She wished she could feel as sure. But if it had been Tony who'd betrayed Dad, would it really help to find that out? Tony and Dad had been friends for years. It would be like Flora finding out that Piotr had betrayed her. It might make him feel much, much worse.

They were stomping through the streets; the wind had died down a little, but it was still freezing. Flora could see her breath mist in front of her, and the colours of the buildings were muted pale and grey by the cold. Sylvie was stamping to keep warm. And because she was in a mood, for some reason.

Flora knew that Sylvie was ready to believe that it was Anna who'd betrayed Dad.

But she couldn't have, could she?

They'd find out soon enough.

'This is Anna's block,' Sylvie said eventually. 'But I don't know which number she's in.' They were standing outside a mansion block apartment building. The red-brick walls looked orange in the late afternoon light; the sculpted turrets looked like something off a Disney castle;

and the fringes of Juliet balconies that ran around the exterior were iron lace.

Last time they'd been here dropping off Anna, Flora had wanted to ask if she could go inside. The building was so pretty, she'd wanted to see if the inside was as nice. But she'd felt too shy, so hadn't asked. It might be too late now.

Andrew walked up the short pathway, lined on either side with bushes ruthlessly clipped into round shapes – a parade of green footballs. 'It's all right,' he said, looking at the Lego-like strip of buzzers, 'the flats have got names on. What's her surname?'

'Van Gulik,' Flora said.

Without hesitation, Andrew pushed the buzzer. They waited. No reply. He pressed again. Long seconds ticked by. Nothing.

'But,' Flora said, 'she's not at work, and she's not with Dad. Where can she be?'

'Shopping?' Andrew suggested.

'She'd be too upset for shopping.'

'Perhaps she lied to the receptionist about being too sick for work,' Sylvie said, a touch too sweetly, Flora thought. What was going on in her sister's head?

Flora checked her watch. It was 4.15 p.m. and getting

darker. Nearly sunset. The temperature was dropping now they were standing still. She pulled her duffel coat tighter. Should they wait? They had no idea where Anna was or when she'd be back.

There was a low wall beside the front door. Andrew was the first to sit, then the others followed suit. The bricks were cold against Flora's legs, even through her woolly tights.

There wasn't much to say, so they sat in silence.

Flora thought about getting her notebook out again, just to make sure she'd recorded everything they'd found out today at Breeze. But it was too cold to bother moving. She could feel it now, weighing down her backpack. It gave her a feeling of being in control, of somehow pinning down facts and events in some sort of order. Placing everything neatly and logically. It was an illusion. She knew that. Sometimes things were just out of control, with no one in charge and no one knowing how they would turn out. But it was good to pretend.

It had been like that when Dad left. For months, everyone pretended that they knew what was happening, while all around them things fell apart. Back then, no one could control the chaos – especially not Mum and Dad. So Flora had started to write things down, to capture moments and look for patterns. She became a scientist of her own life. A specialist in the subject of the Hampshire family. Her diary was her laboratory.

Since meeting Piotr and Andrew and Minnie, her diary had given way to her notebooks – their record of the cases they'd solved. Now, with Dad in a notebook, the Hampshire family were her specialist subject again.

The sky was getting even darker. Street lights fizzed into life. A steady stream of people walked past. Plastic bags, full of last-minute dinner purchases, hung by their sides, banging against work skirts and suit trousers. She could hear the tinny sound of music from too-loud earbuds; idle chatter of people on their phones; the drone of slow-moving traffic.

There was still no sign of Anna.

After twenty minutes, Andrew dropped down off the wall. 'I have to go home,' he said. 'Fish finger sandwiches don't cook themselves.'

With a wave, he was gone.

Another fifteen minutes passed. Then Minnie stood up. 'I have to be home too before it gets too dark,' she said.

Piotr, Sylvie and Flora sat for a while. It was getting colder now that the sun had gone down. The wall was uncomfortable and Flora had pins and needles in her legs. She stood up and jumped painfully.

'How long are we going to wait?' Piotr asked.

Before Flora could answer, a woman came up the pathway towards them. In the gloom, Flora thought for a second that it was Anna, but she realised as soon as the woman got closer that she was too short to be Anna.

The short woman had her head down, rifling through her huge handbag. She wasn't looking where she was going. Her hands moved feverishly. Her foot caught on a loose paving stone and she, and the bag, went flying.

Flora stepped out and grabbed at the woman's arm. She couldn't catch her, but she slowed her fall. Instead of landing face first on the solid ground, the woman managed to take a huge step and just tottered in an ungainly way for a moment. Her hands grabbed at Flora and she hoisted herself up.

Her bag, on the other hand, hit the ground, and everything tumbled from it like a well-struck piñata.

'Oh, rats,' she said.

Piotr and Sylvie helped Flora scoop up all the lost things – notebook and pencil, phone, purse, lipstick, chewing gum, a great jumble of stuff. Last of all was a set of keys.

The woman took them gratefully. 'Oh, thank you.

106

Anna would never forgive me if I'd lost those. Nor would Mr Tumnus.'

'Anna?' Piotr asked.

'Mr Tumnus?' Flora asked.

The woman laughed. 'Yes, I'm feeding my friend Anna's cat while she's away.'

'Anna van Gulik?' Piotr asked.

The woman looked surprised. 'Yes, do you know her?'

'We're waiting for her,' Piotr explained.

'Well, you'll be waiting for her a long time,' the woman said. 'She called me this afternoon. She had to leave in a hurry. It's a good job I already had a key because she didn't have time to meet up.'

'When will she be back?' Flora asked.

The woman shrugged. 'I don't know. If I didn't know any better, I'd say that Anna sounded as though she was in some kind of trouble.'

'Told you so,' Sylvie said softly.

Chapter Sixteen

Flora knew that Minnie and Piotr and Andrew sometimes found Sylvie annoying, but she rarely agreed with them as much as she did right-now-this-minute.

'What are you talking about, Sylvie?' she asked.

Anna's friend had gone into the flat, leaving Flora, Sylvie and Piotr outside in the darkening evening.

In the tangerine light of the street lamp, Flora caught Sylvie's smirk – the telltale twitch at the corner of her mouth.

Sylvie shrugged. 'I tried to tell you, but you didn't listen.'

'What did you try to tell me?'

'That we shouldn't trust Anna.'

'But we know her.' Flora was about to add that they liked her, but she knew she was only talking for herself, so she didn't bother. 'And I told you, she's right-handed. We're looking for a left-handed spook.'

Sylvie hunched her shoulders up to her ears and dropped them in an overly dramatic shrug. 'Well, I don't know. Maybe she's only been pretending to be right-handed all this time to throw us off the scent?'

'That makes about as much sense as a marshmallow saucepan,' Flora said.

Piotr held up both hands, one in the direction of each twin. 'Wait,' he said, 'there's no use fighting over this. Anna's gone. We don't know why, but Flora doesn't think she's the spook and so, for the moment, Tony is still our best suspect. We'll have to find some other way of getting information about him. What about the receptionist? She helped us get into the office; she might help us again.'

That was the best thing about Piotr: he was always ready to look forward, to make new plans, instead of getting upset at the old plans being torn to shreds and stamped on and ground into muck.

But Sylvie was grinning again. 'I don't think we should give up that quickly,' she said. 'I went through Anna's computer while we were in Breeze.'

'Sylvie! Why didn't you tell us before?' Flora felt her cheeks flush red with anger, despite the cold.

Sylvie was wearing her very best butter-wouldn't-melt expression. 'I am telling you now,' she said. 'Anyway, you wouldn't have believed me, even if I had told you what I found. You needed to see that Anna had run away for yourself.'

Flora struggled to squish down her anger. 'Fine, fine,' she said. 'Just tell us. What did you find on Anna's computer?'

'I checked her email; it was all boring. But her browsing history was very interesting. Yesterday afternoon she was looking at hotel websites. Specifically, the Ash Tree.'

'A hotel? I don't understand. Why would Anna be looking at a hotel?' Flora felt a hard knot form in her stomach. Sylvie wasn't right about Anna, was she?

'I imagine that she doesn't want to be found. Maybe she realised that Wendell Shtick was on to her and she's gone into hiding?' Sylvie smiled, though her eyes were steely. 'But I found her.'

'Well,' Flora said desperately, 'you haven't actually found her, just her internet history. She might have been looking at the hotel website to make up for the cancelled holiday.'

'Who goes on holiday in the town they live in?' Sylvie asked witheringly.

'We should go and check it out,' Piotr said, attempting to avert a fight.

Flora gave Piotr a weak smile. She couldn't believe that Sylvie was right. But why else would Anna have run away?

Chapter Seventeen

'Can we go to the hotel now?' Flora asked. She really, really wanted the knot in her stomach to go away, and only talking to Anna was going to do that.

'It's too late to check it out tonight,' Piotr said. 'My mum will be wondering where I am.'

It was true. The temperature had dropped and Flora's fingertips were tingling with the cold, even with her mittens. Mum would be back from work soon. It was probably best if she didn't know that they hadn't spent all day at Breeze.

'I want to go there now,' Sylvie said.

'We should wait until tomorrow,' Flora said. Sylvie was so charged, she'd go in there like a firework, shooting off in all directions. Someone would get hurt. 'We should get home. Mum will worry. You haven't done a blood test today.'

Sylvie made a disgusted noise, but shoved her hands deep into her pockets in defeat.

'Listen, Piotr,' Flora said, 'do you think you could ask your mum to call our mum? If we get permission we can spend the whole day with you tomorrow.'

Piotr nodded. 'Mum would love to see you anyway, she thinks you're brilliant.'

Flora flushed again. Sylvie stomped past the football bushes, now black in the darkness, on to the street.

Sylvie walked ahead. Her hair was tied in a ponytail and its end twitched with every step she took. Flora followed with Piotr.

'Is she all right?' he whispered.

'Not usually,' Flora replied with a smile.

Sylvie waited at the point where Piotr turned off towards his block of flats. She said a curt goodbye. Flora thanked him for waiting in the dark with them at Anna's flat.

She hoped she'd be seeing him in the morning – if Mum agreed.

The twins followed Marsh Road. The market was all packed up. The few people about had heads hidden by hats and hoods, huddled against the chill of the evening.

Flora waited to see whether Sylvie was going to speak. She didn't say a word.

Flora sighed. She was going to have to be the bigger twin, despite being the younger one by a few minutes.

'Are you cross because we didn't go to the hotel?' she asked.

Sylvie's chin shot up into the air. Flora thought she wasn't going to answer, but then she said, 'I'm not cross, I'm furious. We've got an idea where Anna is, but who knows how long she's going to stay there? She might be checking out right now, and the trail will go cold. I can't believe you're making us go straight home, like six-year-olds after nursery.'

Flora decided not to point out that six-year-olds were too big for nursery. They'd reached the theatre square. The grassy space surrounded by plane trees looked sinister in the dark, as though thieves or ogres might be crouched in the shadows. It was too early for the lights around the theatre to come on, or the fairy lights that sparkled in the trees. All the magic was gone and it was just black space left behind.

They turned away from the square towards home.

'Do you remember the first time we met Anna?' Flora asked.

'Of course,' Sylvie snapped. 'It was only a few months ago.'

It had been summer and Dad had told them that he wanted them to meet someone special. He'd driven to fetch them, and then collected Anna. She waited for them outside her flat with an enormous picnic all ready. A wicker basket that was almost too heavy to lift. Like something from an old novel, the wicker creaked and squeaked as Dad hoisted it into the boot. Anna climbed into the front seat with a shy smile for the pair of them. Then got out again because she'd left her sun hat on the roof of the car.

'Do you remember what was in the picnic she made?' Flora asked.

Sylvie's reply was just a grumpy noise, which Flora knew meant she could remember.

'All of our favourite food,' Flora insisted. 'Cheese and pickle sandwiches for me, egg for you, beef and mustard for Dad. She'd made little cupcakes with ballet shoes for you and magnifying glasses for me. And Dad got mini bikes on his. She'd even got some diabetic chocolate in case you weren't supposed to eat cupcakes. She'd asked Dad all about us.'

'I remember,' Sylvie said.

'Would someone who's as nice as that deliberately hurt Dad?'

They were at their door. Sylvie put her key in the lock and went inside. The hall light had come on on a timer, but the rest of the house was in darkness. Mum wasn't back yet. 'It's all very well saying that,' Sylvie said, hanging her coat on the rack and shoving her mittens over the radiator, 'but she *has* hurt him, hasn't she? You saw the state of him. He smelled weird.'

It was true. He had smelled weird.

Flora hung up her own coat and scarf. 'That was only a little bit to do with Anna though, wasn't it? He'd never have been as bad as that if Breeze wasn't in trouble. You know that's what he really cares about.'

Sylvie laughed suddenly. 'Mum does say it's his third child. Can you imagine if we really had a younger brother called Breeze Hampshire who spent his whole time making bikes and scooters?'

'Bree-eeze! Leave that spanner, dinner's ready!' Flora said with a laugh.

'Bree-eeze, have you been in our room and left muddy footprints everywhere?' Sylvie giggled.

As Flora followed her sister into the kitchen, she couldn't help but feel that Dad did behave as though Breeze was a real person to worry over.

He'd be destroyed if he had to leave it.

Chapter Eighteen

Piotr was as good as his word, and his mother called that evening to invite the twins over. Mum accepted with relief. So the following morning, Flora, Sylvie, Piotr, Minnie and Andrew met across the road from the Ash Tree Hotel.

Its white stone walls had greyed over the years to the colour of pavement snow. Its windows were dark and the red awning above the door looked like a frown. It was as welcoming as cold porridge.

They weren't the only ones who had arrived.

'Look,' Andrew said, nudging Flora.

In a battered old car whose paintwork was gently flaking with rust and whose tyres were sprayed with mud was Wendell Shtick. He held a takeaway coffee cup in his right hand and fiddled with his car radio with his left, while half-watching the hotel door.

'What's he doing here?' Minnie asked.

'I imagine the same as us,' Flora replied. 'Looking for Anna.'

'Why hasn't he gone inside to look for her?' Andrew said.

It was odd. Why sit in the car, waiting, when he could just go right in? Then Flora understood. 'I think she must be booked in under a fake name. So he doesn't know which room she's staying in. Unless he knocks on every single door in the hotel, he has no way to find her. All he can do is sit and hope to catch her if she comes in or out.'

The gang looked at each other miserably. If Wendell couldn't find Anna, would they fare any better?

'Unless . . .' Flora said.

'What?' Piotr looked interested.

'Well, I know Anna a bit better than Wendell does. He's never even met her.' Flora smiled. 'Do you think you can distract Wendell while I go into the hotel?'

Andrew grinned. 'I expect we can manage.'

'I'm coming with you!' Sylvie said hotly.

Flora really didn't think that was a good idea. But she knew there was no point rowing about it. A scene in the street would draw Wendell's attention in entirely the wrong way. 'Fine,' she said, 'but please, let me do the talking.'

Andrew, Piotr and Minnie strolled casually up to Wendell's car. Flora watched carefully, waiting for her moment to run across the street and into the hotel.

Andrew gave a theatrical gasp and started tapping at the car window. It rolled down and Wendell growled, 'What do you want?'

'I thought it was you!' Andrew gushed. 'Are you on a stake-out? Can we help? I'm really good at watching. Though I can sometimes talk too much, can't I, Piotr?'

'Oh, yes. He can watch. But he can talk too. He should be on the telly.'

'I will be one day,' Andrew said. 'I'll have my own show. You can come on it, if you like. You could tell everyone about the time we did a stake-out together.'

'Go away!' Wendell snapped.

'If you don't want us to do the stake-out with you,' Minnie said, 'maybe we could run errands? Fetch dough-nuts, coffee, that sort of thing? We could be, like, your assistants.'

Wendell yelled a great many rude words, and waved his coffee angrily.

He wasn't watching the hotel front at all.

Flora grabbed Sylvie's hand, checked the road, and

then raced across. Up the steps. Through the revolving door. Into the lobby. Expecting a shout behind them at any moment. But the shout didn't come.

They were in.

Flora's heart was beating a quickstep as she looked around. The wooden revolving door, with its brass handles and furry brushes to keep out the draught, slowed and stopped. The lobby was spread out before them. It was a wide space, with high ceilings. There were black-and-white tiles on the floor. On the walls, oil paintings of hills and carriages hung under brass lamps. Beyond the lifts, a wooden staircase rose; following the line of the walls, brass poles held the carpet in place. There was a smell of polish and cakes. It would have been nice, if Flora was a bit less terrified of being thrown out.

In the centre of it all was a reception desk. A woman in a neat blue uniform stood behind the desk, tapping at the computer screen in front of her.

Flora tried to calm her jagged pulse as she stepped forward. Sylvie was doing nothing to make her feel better. Flora could see her eyes darting around the lobby, searching out Anna, like a cat looking for a mouse.

Flora reached the desk.

'Hello,' the woman said with a smile.

'Hello,' Flora said. Her mouth was so dry that the word was practically a whisper.

'Can I help?'

'Yes.' Flora nodded. 'I've come to see my friend. She's expecting me.'

She hoped she knew Anna as well as she thought. She hoped her guess was right. 'Lucy,' Flora said, remembering the beloved character in the Narnia books that Anna loved so much. 'Lucy Pevensie.'

The woman behind the desk didn't drop her smile. She tapped her keyboard and peered at the screen. 'Room 36,' she said. 'Up to the third floor and along the corridor. Shall I call her and tell her you're on your way?'

'No, thank you,' Flora said, 'there's no need.'

'Well, you have a nice day.'

'You too.'

Sylvie stalked off first, striding out towards the lift with her arms swinging – battle mode. Flora trotted to catch her up. 'Sylvie!'

Sylvie ignored her. She brought her palm down on the lift call button, once, twice, three times.

The lift pinged open.

They stepped into the space. The mirror on the back wall reflected their twin images – four red-haired,

122

milk-pale girls, splattered with freckles. Two worried, two determined.

'Sylvie!' Flora said again.

Sylvie pressed the button for the third floor firmly.

'Sylvie! You have to let me do the talking. Listen! If you go in there shouting your head off, she'll never tell us anything. Saving Breeze for Dad is more important than winning a shouting match with Anna.'

Sylvie shrugged.

The lift juddered upwards. First floor. Second. Nearly there.

Flora held Sylvie's shoulder and looked right into her eyes. 'Sylvie, if you don't do this my way, Dad might lose everything. Is that what you want?'

Sylvie didn't reply. Flora was shocked to see that her eyes glistened with tears.

'Is it?' she asked again.

'No,' Sylvie whispered. 'I'm angry with him. And at Anna. But that's not what I want.'

'Good. Then follow my lead.' Flora wasn't sure she'd ever spoken to Sylvie like that. It felt . . . odd, but good.

Really good.

The lift doors opened.

A green carpet stretched out in front of them, like a beautifully trimmed lawn. Beige and cream doors punctuated the corridor. Each door had a polished brass plate with the room number engraved in black. 33, 34, 35. There. 36. Flora stood in front of it. She raised her fist to knock.

She paused.

Was this the right thing to do? Anna was in hiding for a reason. Would finding out the reason make things better or worse for Dad?

She didn't know. But she had to find out.

She brought down her fist on the wood.

She heard a rustling sound from inside the room. Someone moving. A cupboard door creaked. Then she heard a chain slide across. The door opened.

Anna's face appeared in the open crack of the doorway. The security chain hung from the door to the wall. The narrow gap was wide enough for Flora to see the terrified look Anna wore. Tears had dried in pale smears on her brown cheeks.

'Flora!' she gasped. 'And . . . and Sylvie!'

'Hello.'

'What are you doing here? How did you find me?'

Flora checked the corridor. It was empty. 'We've come to help,' she said. 'Can we come in?'

The door closed. Flora heard the rattle of the chain. Then the door opened wide. Anna waved them in urgently. They rushed past her and she closed the door behind them.

Anna leaned against the solid wood as though it were the only thing holding her up. 'Please. How did you find me?'

'Search history on your computer,' Flora said.

Anna's face creased in alarm. She looked as tired as Dad had the previous day. She wore no make-up and her hair was pulled back in a simple ponytail. She sat down heavily on the edge of her bed and put her head in her hands. 'If you can find me,' she whispered into her palms, 'then anyone can.'

Flora wondered if she should mention Wendell, watching outside? She would, but not yet. 'Anna, why don't you want anyone to find you?'

Anna bit back a sob. 'Oh, I've been so stupid.'

Flora felt cold. Numb. Sylvie was right. Anna had something serious to hide. Could she really be the spook?

'Please, tell us what's wrong,' Flora said. She could sense Sylvie beside her, desperate to pounce but straining to stop herself.

'I can't,' Anna whispered, 'I'm ashamed.'

Flora felt sick. Her throat tightened.

'Anna,' Sylvie said. Her voice was surprisingly kind. 'If you don't tell us, we'll just imagine the worst. It's better to tell.'

Anna pulled a tissue from her trouser pocket and held it to her face. 'I'm in trouble,' she said.

Flora had to sit. She felt as though the world was constricting, the air was too thick. Was this what it felt like to faint? Was this how Sylvie felt when her blood sugar dropped? She fumbled for the chair that stood in front of the dressing table and fell into it.

'Who are you in trouble with?' Sylvie asked evenly.

Anna hung her head. 'I can't tell you.'

No. Flora couldn't believe it.

Anna was to blame.

Anna had betrayed Dad.

'Tell us,' Sylvie said.

Anna covered her eyes with the tissue. Her voice was just a whisper. 'I mean, I can't tell you because I don't know. I . . . I was threatened. But I don't know who by.'

The buzzing in Flora's ears cleared; the world tightened back into focus. 'What?' she said out loud. 'Anna, you're not making sense.'

Sylvie crossed the plush carpet soundlessly. Flora

heard a tap run in the en suite. Then Sylvie was back. She held a damp flannel, folded neatly and wrung out. She offered it to Anna. Anna stared at it blankly. 'For your face,' Sylvie said. 'Sometimes, when I've cried, Mum makes this for me. It feels nice to clean your face. Fresh start, you know.'

Anna tucked her manky tissue away and took the cold flannel from Sylvie. She held it close to her skin. Then she swiped left and right, across her cheeks, wiping blotchy tears away. She looked a bit better. Stronger. 'Thank you,' she whispered.

Sylvie gave a tight shrug, then went to sit on the far side of the room.

'Start from the beginning,' Flora said.

Anna dropped her hands into her lap. 'You were there,' she said softly. 'You were there when it started. When Daniel cancelled the holiday I went to Breeze instead of the airport. You remember?'

Flora nodded.

Anna barely paused. She seemed eager to tell the whole story now that she had begun. 'It was like sliding into a nightmare. I thought I would take another look at the to-do list for the anniversary party on Saturday. So I opened my emails. And it just pinged into the inbox. This horrible message. It wasn't from a named account, it was just a string of numbers attached to a Gmail address. And it wasn't signed. An anonymous email. It said if I didn't stop what I was working on immediately, leave the company and stay away until after the party, then they'd tell Daniel, they'd tell him . . .' Anna's grip on the flannel tightened and Flora saw beads of water drip on to her lap.

'What? What would they tell him?'

'That I was at Breeze last Saturday. The day the blue-prints went missing,' Anna whispered.

Sylvie leaped from her chair, making them all jump. 'Were you? Why? What were you doing there?'

'I can't tell you.'

'But you admit you were there? You were in the office at the exact same time that the safe was opened?'

'I was. But in my office, not Daniel's.'

'Did you see anything? Did you see the spook?' Flora asked.

Anna shook her head sadly. 'I didn't notice a thing. But the anonymous email said that they'd noticed me. I was . . . I was singing, you see. In the corridor. They must have heard me.'

'What were you doing?' Sylvie snapped.

'*The Sound of Music*,' Anna replied.

128

'No. Not the songs. What were you doing there in the first place?'

Anna's shoulders curled tight, her arms crossed over her front. She was going to cry again. 'I can't say, but I promise, I had nothing to do with the theft.'

Flora couldn't stand it any more. She scooted from her seat on to the bed and threw a protective arm around Anna. She squeezed her tight and whispered that it was all going to be OK. Sylvie sat back down in her own chair. Then she tutted and launched herself upright again. This time she took the kettle into the bathroom and filled it. She rattled teacups and spiked single serves of long-life milk while she waited for it to boil.

By the time Sylvie had made tea for them all, Flora had soothed Anna enough to take the proffered cup.

They sipped in silence for a moment. Then Flora said, 'I think the crucial thing here is that there's someone who needs to get you out of the way. It's strange that they mentioned your work. Why would they say you had to stop what you were doing? It's as though you leaving the building wasn't enough. They needed you to abandon your work too.'

Anna wiped her eyes. She looked thoughtful, interested now. There was more colour in her cheeks.

'What were you working on?' Sylvie asked, glaring through the steam of her teacup.

'The party, mostly. Guest lists, catering. Janyce was in charge and she wanted everything to run smoothly. It was more like a royal wedding than an office party.'

'What were you going to do before the nasty email arrived?'

'Janyce had asked for some changes to the promo video. It's a sort of fun history of the company. Photos of the partners as kids, footage of tests gone wrong, people falling off bikes, things like that. Nothing serious. It was going to go up on the screens around the party. But Janyce didn't like the photos I'd used of her. Said they made her look like a nerd. So I was going to change them.'

Flora pinched the arm of her chair tightly. If the spook wanted to keep that video off the screens, well then, they *had* to see it. 'Where is it now?' she asked. 'Have you got a copy?'

Anna shook her head. 'It's all on my computer at work. Backed up to the company servers.'

'Well, it shouldn't be too hard to take a look,' Sylvie said.

'It wouldn't if you hadn't got us banned from Breeze, remember?' Flora replied.

That reminded Flora of an uncomfortable fact. Wendell.

She had to tell Anna.

'Breeze have got a PI looking into the stolen blue-prints,' she said sadly. 'His name is Wendell Shtick. I'm sorry, but he thinks you stole them.'

'Me?' Anna's dark eyes flashed wide.

'Sorry. And he knows you're in here. He's watching the front door. I think someone might be trying to set you up.'

'Who?' Anna whispered.

'The same person who is trying to destroy my dad,' Flora replied.

And Tony Valeti was their prime suspect.

Chapter Nineteen

Wendell Shtick was in his car, bent over the steering wheel, howling in pain, when Flora and Sylvie left the hotel. Andrew was holding an empty coffee cup. Minnie was trying to pass some dubious-looking napkins through the open window. Wendell ignored the napkins; instead he bounced up and down in his seat, like a toddler strapped in against its will.

'I think Andrew's done enough distracting for today,' Flora said, suddenly feeling very sorry for Wendell.

As they got closer, Wendell's howls became wet sobs.

'I'm so sorry, Mr Shtick,' Andrew said. 'I've never seen coffee leap so high. It's like some kind of world record. Do you want me to see if I can get some clean trousers for you? There might be Lost Property in that hotel over there.'

'Just leave me alone, leave me alone,' Wendell whimpered.

'OK. Sorry again. Thanks for the stake-out!' Andrew said cheerfully.

Piotr was shaking his head as Flora and Sylvie joined the others. 'Andrew scalded the PI.'

'It was an accident,' Andrew said. 'Honest. I was trying to show him how to get a suspect into a headlock. The coffee thing just . . . happened.'

They left the battered car and the broken PI to it and headed back towards Marsh Road.

Sylvie was silent.

It was left to Flora to explain to the others what they'd found out. She told them about the malicious email, and the fact that the spook hadn't simply stolen the blue-prints, but that he had blackmailed Anna too.

'And she admitted that she was at Breeze the day the safe was opened?' Minnie asked.

'Yes, but she won't tell us why,' Sylvie said, with acid in her voice.

Flora slowed down. She let the others walk ahead – Minnie with her arms swinging at every stride; Andrew bouncing from paving slab to paving slab, unwilling to step on any cracks; Piotr, who strolled thoughtfully, his thumbs looped in his pockets. But as Sylvie passed, Flora reached out and took her arm. She slipped her hand through the crook of her sister's elbow. Sylvie's body felt stiff and angled, an angry triangle.

Flora leaned in closer, so that their foreheads were nearly touching. 'I know you don't want to trust Anna,' she whispered gently, 'but you have to start trusting people again sometime, you know.'

'I do trust people. Well, you and Piotr.'

'I think we can trust Anna, I really do.'

Sylvie didn't reply.

Chapter Twenty

'I can't keep imposing on Mrs Domek,' Mum said firmly. They were home again. Mum was back from work and already worrying about arrangements for the following day.

'But Mum,' Flora said, 'she doesn't mind, she likes us.'

Mum picked up a pile of folders with a sigh and dropped them into her briefcase. Flora swished side to side on Mum's office chair. She didn't know where Sylvie had got to. She was maybe upstairs in her room deciding whether or not to believe Anna's story.

'It isn't right.' Mum sounded tired. 'We can't rely on other people to look after you. I'm going to call the agency again. I'll see if someone can come for the last couple of days before the weekend.'

'Dad can do it!' Flora said.

'With all that's happening at Breeze? He can't keep you and that company in his head at the same time; he'll be hopelessly distracted. I thought I read something in the news about a big board meeting being called.' Mum looked at a grey folder, then switched it for a red one from her filing cabinet.

'He's at home,' Flora said, watching Mum's face carefully. If Mum thought that Dad was sloping around at home when he was supposed to be on holiday with the twins, then she'd be really cross. 'I think he's a bit poorly,' Flora added.

'Is he?' Mum snapped the clasps on her case closed. 'Well, he'll hardly be able to look after the two of you, then, will he?'

'We'll look after him,' Flora said. She made sure that she kept any hint of a whine out of her voice – Mum was much more likely to respond to reason than moaning. 'Sylvie and I aren't old enough to stay on our own, I agree,' Flora said.

Mum's mouth twitched. 'That's good of you.'

'But we are old enough to be in the house with a responsible adult who's a bit under the weather. We'll all sit under duvets on the sofa and watch his DVD copy of *It's a Wonderful Life*. That's all.'

Mum's twitch became a grin. 'I wish I could do that tomorrow. It sounds nice.'

'Doesn't it? You can't deny us a small treat like that, not during school holidays. It would be entirely too cruel.'

Mum picked up her case, being careful not to scratch the polished surface of her desk. 'Cruel? When did you get so cheeky?' She laughed. 'Fine, you win. But don't go catching his germs. Keep your distance. I don't want you off sick next week too.'

'Thanks!' Flora gave Mum a quick hug, almost knocking her off her poised axis. Then she rushed upstairs to find Sylvie.

Sylvie was lying back on her bed, staring up at the ceiling.

'We aren't getting a stupid childminder tomorrow,' Flora said, 'we're going to Dad's.'

'What about finding out what Anna was working on?' Sylvie said flatly.

'We can't get into Breeze without a responsible adult. Wendell Shtick has banned us, you know that. But Dad can get in. If he's well enough. If we help him get better then he can get us into the office, and into Anna's computer.'

'Hmm.' Sylvie sounded listless, as though her batteries had run out.

'Come on,' Flora insisted, 'shake a leg.'

Sylvie waggled her right leg a bit, but didn't get up.

'What's the matter?' Flora asked, coming into the room properly.

'Nothing,' Sylvie said, in a voice that really meant *something*.

'Tell me.'

'I'm just worried about Dad. Do you think Anna will go back to him?'

'I don't know.'

'Do you think . . . do you think it's my fault if she doesn't?' Sylvie sounded small, frightened even. Not at all like the regular Sylvie that Flora was used to. It was odd. Unnerving.

'Of course it's not your fault,' Flora said. 'She'll think it's the fault of the two-faced, scheming, no-good dumb-bell who sent her the nasty email. Who tried to frame her for the theft. Who made her hide away. I think she'll blame them, don't you?'

Sylvie chuckled a little. 'Well,' she said, 'when you put it like that.'

'So, are we agreed? First thing in the morning we'll go to Dad's and get him to take us to Breeze? Then we can find out what was in Anna's video that threatened Tony so badly?'

'Agreed,' Sylvie said firmly.

Chapter Twenty-One

Mum dropped them off outside Dad's. Flora rummaged for her key and let them both in. They raced up the stairs to the top floor.

Dad's house smelled funny, as though someone had spilled milk and not bothered to wipe it up. She could see straight down the hallway to the kitchen at the end. From here it was clear that Dad's usually immaculate kitchen was piled with washing-up: dirty plates and bowls and a stack of takeaway cartons.

'Dad?' Flora called.

'Flora?' Dad's voice came from the back of the flat. Flora wrinkled her nose against the smell and headed towards the kitchen, with Sylvie following behind making dramatic gagging noises.

Dad wasn't in the kitchen. But the reef of dirty plates suggested he'd been spending way too much time at home.

'Dad?' Flora said again.

'Here.'

He was tucked into the biggish alcove that he used as a home office. He sat bundled under a rug in the battered armchair that was placed under the window. The stubble on his chin and cheeks was thick enough to almost count as a beard. He was wearing clothes that might have been old gym gear, or makeshift pyjamas, it was hard to tell. Whatever they were, they were all about comfort and not at all about style.

'Hi, Dad,' Flora said.

'Flora, sweetheart, what are you two doing here?'

'Mum rang. Don't you remember?'

'Oh. Oh, yes.' He glanced at his phone, which was resting on his cluttered, untidy desk. 'I was about to clear up. But I haven't quite got around to it.'

'She called, like, an hour ago,' Sylvie snapped. 'Are you going to work today? Can we come with you?'

Dad gazed out of the window. There was a tree whose branches reached as far as the pane of glass. In summer, its leaves rustled like the pages of a book. Today, the twigs were bare.

'Dad!' Sylvie said.

'Oh, sorry. No, I'm not going in today.'

'You should wash up, then. The flat smells like eggy armpits.'

Flora put her hand on Sylvie's arm.

'Has something happened?' Flora asked. 'I mean . . . something besides Anna?'

'And the spook?' Sylvie added. 'And the blueprints?'

Dad pulled the rug higher over his gym-gear-slash-pyjamas. The rug was too small; his feet popped out the bottom.

'Nothing's happened,' Dad said softly.

'Do you need anything?' Flora offered. 'Coffee? A sandwich?' If Andrew could make fish finger sandwiches then so could she.

'I'm fine, love,' he said. 'It isn't your job to listen to my problems.'

Flora couldn't help wondering whose job it was. Who did Dad go to when he needed some sympathy? Who listened to him in the way that Sylvie, or Mum, or Piotr and the others would listen to her? Who, at the end of a difficult day, did Dad share with? With Anna gone, he had no one. It wasn't right.

Tony had taken that from him.

'What about the party?' Sylvie asked Dad. 'It's the day after tomorrow. You're going to that, aren't you?'

Dad watched the tree for a while. Then he said, 'I don't really feel like going out.'

'But the party was why we were only going on holiday for five days! The whole reason why you didn't want to take the whole half-term! We were coming back from the beach and the sun and the fun early so that you could go to the stupid party, and now you can't even cross town to go to it?'

Dad shrugged.

Sylvie's face had turned a shade of red that was somewhere between pillar box and strawberry.

Flora sighed.

Sylvie heard her. 'Don't you pretend that you're not bothered either!'

'I'm not.' Flora held up her hands. 'I just don't want to get all ranty.'

'Ranty!' Sylvie yelled. 'How can I be ranty? That's not even a real word!'

'Girls,' Dad said gently. 'I won't be going to the party because the board has agreed to meet then. They'll all be there, dressed up in their finery, and they'll all sit down at 7 p.m. to talk about me, and then, at 7.30 p.m. they'll vote and it will all be over. I don't think I'll be feeling much like a party at that point.'

'Over?' Flora asked.

'They'll vote on whether I'm fit to stay on at Breeze. And as the blueprints were wholly my responsibility, I expect they'll vote no.

'And anyway,' Dad added, 'I've got no one to go with.'

Flora gestured at Sylvie to follow her back out to the kitchen. The grimy water was a bit eggy-armpit, she had to admit. She pulled open the dishwasher and started putting the dirty plates inside.

Sylvie lifted Dad's dressing gown off a chair and dropped it on the floor. She sat down.

Flora picked up the dressing gown and folded it before putting it on the table.

'Well,' Sylvie said, 'what are we going to do?'

'I can tidy the kitchen. Maybe you could see if he's got any clean shirts?'

'Not about the flat!' Sylvie said. 'About Anna. Her computer. The spook. The plan was to get Dad to take us to Breeze so that we could check out her video.'

'I know. But one step at a time. Let's get him clean and dressed before we try to save his job.'

'Dad will be fine,' Sylvie said. 'He's a grown-up.'

'But that doesn't mean he'll be OK. I feel so bad for

him.' Flora collected some of the greasy fried chicken boxes from the counter and carried them to the bin. She stepped on the lever, and realised the reason the boxes were on the counter was because the bin was full. She put the containers on the floor for a moment and grabbed the bin handles. She heaved. The heavy bin liner didn't shift. She couldn't lift it. She let the lid drop.

'Pass me an empty bin bag, they're in that drawer,' Flora said.

Sylvie opened a few drawers, poking around sandwich bags and bottle openers and things for recorking wine bottles.

'Not that one, the one below.'

Sylvie finally found the roll and tore off an empty bag. She held it open with a look of absolute disgust as Flora tipped in the greasy containers.

'Why do you feel bad?' Sylvie asked. 'None of this is your fault.'

'It feels a bit like it is. Not the spook, of course, but Dad not having anyone to look after him when he's like this.'

'That's nothing to do with us.'

'We left,' Flora said.

'No. Mum left, and took us with her. That's different.

144

And she says she had to leave because nothing mattered to Dad that wasn't engineered.'

Flora didn't know what to else to say. Mum said that Breeze had been everything to Dad; more important than Sylvie's performances or Flora's school reports, more important than parents' evenings, or birthday parties, or reading them bedtime stories.

And now it was being taken from him.

He'd be nothing without Breeze.

Even if they did prove that it was Tony who had stolen the blueprints, that wouldn't make Dad feel better. Not if the board voted to kick him out.

Flora tied a knot in the top of the new rubbish bag and put it beside the bin.

'It might be my fault that Anna's gone, though,' Sylvie said warily. 'I was never very nice to her.'

Flora didn't argue. But she gave Sylvie a sympathetic smile. 'Maybe Wendell Shtick will realise that it wasn't Anna who's the spook and he'll sort it all out before the board meets. And maybe Anna will come back.'

'Wendell Shtick couldn't find his way out of a paper bag,' Sylvie said scornfully. 'Even if he had directions.'

Sylvie was right. Wendell wasn't going to be the one to make life all rainbows and unicorns.

It was up to them. They had to stop the board from taking Breeze away from Dad. They had forty-eight hours to solve it all. Forty-eight hours to give Dad hope.

But Flora had no idea how they were going to do it.

Chapter Twenty-Two

Dad stayed in his study. No matter how Sylvie scolded, or Flora coaxed, he stayed in his battered old chair, watching the wind in the trees.

There was no way that he was going to go with them to Breeze. He wasn't even going to shave anytime soon.

And they couldn't just walk in past reception, not without an adult – Wendell Shtick had made sure of that.

They couldn't ask Anna to go with them; she was too frightened of the blackmailer.

And asking Mum was no good; she'd hit the roof if she realised just how much time the twins had spent not being watched by Mr and Mrs Domek that week.

'Could we break in?' Sylvie wondered.

'Not while they're so worried about thieves and spooks,' Flora said. 'Anyway, the workshop doesn't have windows so people can't look in, and the offices are all full of people. We'd be spotted in a heartbeat.'

'What about at night?' Sylvie wondered.

'Alarms, CCTV, locked doors. Last time I checked, I wasn't a ninja.'

'What we need is just to be able to walk in, blend in with the crowd, act as if we totally belong there ...' Sylvie trailed off.

'What?' Flora asked.

Sylvie dashed across the kitchen. She opened a drawer and pulled out a pizza delivery leaflet.

'Sylvie!' Flora couldn't help but shout.

'What?'

'This is serious. Dad needs help, not pizzas.'

Sylvie glared at Flora. Flora so often wilted under that stare, like a basil plant in midday sun, but not today. She didn't care if Sylvie was worried about her blood sugar, or craving carbs, or was just simply hungry. Pizza wasn't the answer to their problems.

'Flora,' Sylvie said, 'I am not thinking about food.' She tossed the leaflet aside and reached into the drawer again. 'I am thinking about a way to get us into Breeze without Wendell Shtick finding out.' She pulled another leaflet – an advert for double-glazing – from the drawer, and then a thick square of cream cardboard. A thick square of cream cardboard with words printed clearly on it – *An Invitation to the Breeze Masked Ball.*

Sylvie held the invitation in front of her chest like a judge awarding a score. Then she raised an expectant eyebrow.

Flora read the eyebrow clearly. 'Sorry,' she muttered.

'Pardon?' Sylvie cupped her free hand around her ear.

'Sorry. But that's two apologies. You're not getting another.'

Sylvie smirked, then handed the card over.

Flora read the rest of the twirling black writing.

You and a guest are cordially invited to celebrate the tenth anniversary of Breeze at company headquarters on February 17th from 7 p.m.
Dress Code: Black tie masquerade.

'It says it's for two people,' Flora said. 'That's not enough for all of us.'

'Well, two of us will go in and open a window or fire escape or something, and let the others in. The offices will be empty, but the alarms won't be switched on with all the crowds of people there. Mum will let us go if she thinks Dad will be there We'll gatecrash the ball!'

'Like Cinderella,' Flora said, smiling.

'Like disco ninjas,' Sylvie replied.

Chapter Twenty-Three

As if they were in a fairy tale, they were going to need clothes to wear to the ball. The twins had a few nice dresses in their wardrobe, but they had no masks, and no black tie outfits for Piotr and Andrew. And no fairy godmother to wave a wand over any handy rodents.

'Maybe they own black tie already?' Flora said doubtfully.

'I'll call Piotr,' Sylvie said, with a faint blush. She dialled and spoke to his mum, who asked after them and Mum and Dad before putting Piotr on.

'Hello,' he said.

'It's Sylvie. Have you got black tie?'

'A black tie? No, my school one is green.'

'No,' Sylvie said, 'not *a* black tie. Black tie. It means formal clothes, preferably a tuxedo.'

'A tuxedo? One of those suits with flappy bits at the back and a bow tie?'

'Yes.'

'Why on earth would I own one of those? I'm not a stage magician.'

'Can you get one? Tonight? Or tomorrow? And one for Andrew too?'

'What? What's this about?'

Sylvie grinned at her phone. 'We're going to a party.'

'And we're the clowns?'

'No! We're guests. Well, two of us will be. The other three will be gatecrashers. But well-dressed gatecrashers. So you'll get a tuxedo?'

'No. Wait. Andrew's here.' The phone was muffled for a moment, as Piotr spoke to Andrew. Then Piotr was back. 'Andrew doesn't have a black tie either. And we have no idea where to get one, and no money. And to be honest, I don't want to look like a penguin, thanks very much.'

Sylvie covered the mouthpiece and looked at Flora. 'He says no,' she said.

Flora took the phone. 'Piotr? It's Flora. Listen, this is really, really important. It's our one chance to get inside Breeze and find out what's really going on.'

'Disguised as penguins?' Piotr said.

'In masks,' Flora replied.

'I've got a Spider-Man mask I could wear. And I'll wear my best jeans. Will that do?'

Flora was fairly certain that jeans and a Spider-Man mask would get them thrown out quicker than you could say 'Let me see your invitations again, miss'. It wasn't going to work. Sylvie must have seen the panic on Flora's face, because she snatched back the phone.

There was more kerfuffle as Andrew took the phone from Piotr. 'Why are we dressing as penguins? Is it fancy dress?' he asked breathlessly. 'Can I come as a salt-and-vinegar crisp? I've got some yellow foam. It used to be a cushion, but I broke it.'

'No!' Sylvie insisted. How had she ended up going to a party with Spider-Boy and his amazing salted snacks? 'No! No costumes. I'll get you something to wear. And you *will* wear it. And you will *not* moan. Is that clear?'

Andrew swallowed. 'Crystal.'

'Good. Meet at the cafe. Tomorrow morning. Tell Piotr. And Minnie,' Sylvie added reluctantly. Then she hung up.

'Where are we going to get tuxedos from?' Flora asked.

'You'll see.'

* * *

Mum let them go to Mrs Domek's the following day. But Sylvie and Flora didn't go to Piotr's flat – the cafe was much more convenient for what Sylvie had in mind.

Andrew and Piotr were already there. Minnie dashed in moments behind them. 'So,' Minnie said, 'the boys need penguin costumes and we're dressing as Spider-Men, is that right?'

Flora raised her eyes to the ceiling. Trusting Andrew with a message was like yelling it at a speeding car and hoping the driver heard. 'No, not exactly,' she replied.

'We're going to the theatre,' Sylvie said with a smile.

Flora hadn't been to the theatre for a while. It was in the square beyond Marsh Road, and had been the location of their very first mystery, when the gang had uncovered a plot to steal a diamond necklace. Sylvie was there often, though, as part of stage school. So she led the way.

'Why are we going to the theatre?' Andrew asked.

Flora just smiled – he'd see!

When they'd solved their first case, Piotr's dad had been working on the stage door, but he'd left to train as a special constable, so now it was only Sylvie who recognised the security guard. She gave him a beaming smile – Flora recognised it as the one she used when she was after something. And sure enough, the guard was soon ringing Nita up in props and arranging for her to meet them outside Wardrobe.

They all knew the way – through the lobby and up two flights of stairs.

Nita, the stage manager, had been kind to them before, and Flora was hoping she would be kind to them now.

She was waiting at the top of the staircase. She swivelled towards them in her black pumps. The rest of her outfit, scarf down to socks, was black too – she was always ready to dash about in the theatre wings, unseen by the audience.

'The Hampshire twins!' Nita said warmly. 'And Piotr and Andrew and Minnie. How lovely! Though I imagine this isn't a casual visit. What is it this time? Investigating stolen rubies? Searching for long-lost treasure?'

'Nope,' Flora said with a smile, 'we're stopping a spook who's ruining Dad's business.'

Nita nodded, her brown eyes sparkling with delight. 'Of course you are. And what can a humble stage manager do to help?'

'Well,' Sylvie said, 'we need a couple of miniature tuxedos. And some masks.'

Nita laughed and said, 'Well, you might be in luck.

Wendy isn't in yet.' Wendy was the totally terrifying wardrobe mistress. 'But actually, even if she was, I think she's still so grateful to you for saving the theatre's reputation that she'd let you borrow anything.'

'Are you sure?' Flora said. Wendy wasn't known for being warm. In fact, her reputation was more frosty, freezing and ferocious.

'Oh yes,' Nita said, 'she's mellowed. Come on in.'

The wardrobe and prop store was as wondrous as Flora remembered – ranks and rows of outfits in every colour under the sun. Shelves of hats, boxes of gloves and neckties and bags and jewellery. The musty smell of old clothes, guarded against moths with camphor and lavender.

'Boys' clothes?' Nita checked. 'Over here.' There was a long rail with chimney sweeps' rags, princes' velvets, gangsters' hoodies, a hundred lifetimes' worth of clothes, set against a far wall. Nita flicked through the hangers. 'Andrew, Piotr, come here. Have you grown?'

'Piotr has,' Minnie said. 'Andrew, not so much.'

'Hey!' Andrew said indignantly.

'Here!' Nita lifted off two outfits. Perfectly cut black trousers and jackets, with a gleaming white shirt and white bow tie underneath. 'This do you?' She held them against the boys' fronts to see if they would fit.

Flora felt that she was looking at their tickets to the ball. 'Nita, you're amazing!' she said.

'What on earth is going on?' said a familiar, fear-inducing, marrow-freezing voice. Wendy. Standing in the doorway with a scowl fixed to her face as though it had been nailed there. She stomped into the room. As she got closer, she peered at the unwelcome intruders . . . and smiled!

Flora could not remember seeing Wendy smile before. It was like seeing a shark wearing a top hat – totally unexpected and a little bit creepy.

'My favourite gang!' Wendy gushed. 'The fab five – like the Beatles with one extra.' Wendy laughed. An actual laugh! Flora looked at Sylvie in alarm.

'They need disguises for their latest investigation,' Nita said quickly. 'I hope you don't mind?'

'Mind? Of course not!' Wendy said. 'Unless they come back with a single stain, or tear, or splatter of mud. In which case, I'll tan your hides and have your guts for garters. Is that clear?'

'Clear,' Piotr agreed.

'Splendid!' Wendy said, with another shark-toothed smile. 'Well, good luck with your enquiries.'

Nita wrapped one arm around the shoulders of each

twin and scooted them across the huge storeroom towards props – away from Wendy. 'She's mellowed,' Nita whispered, 'but not thawed all the way through.'

Flora held on tight to the tuxedos, in case Wendy changed her mind.

'Masks!' Nita said, and stopped in front of the stack of shelves that were filled with some of the best masks Flora had ever seen – gold-and-red Venetian masks with hooked noses and dark ribbons; cat masks with whiskers; clowns and criminals; presidents and princesses; even something that looked a lot like a Ninja Turtle. She really hoped Andrew didn't spot that one. She moved a Cyberman head in front of it, just in case. Then she took down an ornate Venetian mask. Its almond-shaped eyeholes were dark, eerie. Gold glitter swirled across its cheeks; blood-red ribbons dripped down its sides. It was perfect.

'That's one of a set,' Nita said. She handed similar masks to the others, all the same spooky porcelain shape but decorated in different colours: black, purple, green, blue. They were magical.

'Are you sure we can borrow these?' Flora asked.

'Yes,' Nita said, 'of course. Just bring them back when you're done.'

They were about to leave when Minnie paused. There

was a look on her face that Flora didn't quite understand. She looked sad, but happy too. It was a look of longing.

'What is it?' Nita asked kindly.

'Well,' Minnie said softly. 'The boys are going to look good. And Flora and Sylvie have party dresses. But my best dress is too small for me now. It looks stupid. I was wondering . . .' She bit her lip.

Nita reached out and gave her arm a quick squeeze. 'You'd like something glamorous to wear?'

Minnie gave a tiny, slight nod. Her grin was more embarrassed than anything.

'No problem. You're a young lady now,' Nita said. 'It's only right you should look the part. You can choose what you like.'

Minnie's grin became a full-blown, high-watt smile, as though Nita had told her Christmas was rescheduled and was happening tomorrow.

'Me too,' Sylvie said. 'My party dress is old.'

Flora thought of the beautiful dresses on the hangers in Wardrobe and nodded sheepishly. 'Me too, please, if you don't mind?' she said.

Nita laughed. 'I think we can manage that.'

Chapter Twenty-Four

The next evening, they all met at Minnie's mum's salon to get ready. The wall of mirrors in front of the salon chairs was very useful – they spun and twirled and laughed at their own reflections.

But Minnie looked the most amazing – though Flora had no intention of telling Sylvie that.

Nita had given them all great clothes. But Minnie's was a proper, grown-up-sized ball gown. She was just about tall enough to wear it. It was purple silk that shimmered like water. She had a fake fur wrap to go over it to keep out the chill.

She looked like a billion-squillion dollars.

The rest of them weren't bad either.

Andrew smoothed down the tails of his jacket and readjusted his bow tie for the hundredth time. 'I look like I could be in one of those old black-and-white films,' he said, swinging jazz hands around his head. He attempted a tap shuffle, but just managed to get his feet tangled in each other.

'Careful!' Flora said, catching him before he fell. 'Never forget that the clothes we're wearing belong to Wendy! Are you ready to explain to her why there's a hole where there shouldn't be?'

Andrew sobered up immediately.

Flora and Sylvie wore party dresses too – they were chiffoned and sequinned like glittering presents.

Everyone was ready for the ball.

They walked together up towards the industrial estate, and Breeze. Flora felt like something from the pages of a story, lighter than air in her drape of green lace. She had to force herself to remember that she wasn't there to enjoy herself. She was there to find proof that Tony had betrayed Dad.

Sylvie led the way to the party. The front of the building looked enchanted in the wintry evening – fairy lights festooned the entrance; lanterns were dotted enticingly on either side of the path. A slow stream of people were making their way towards the door, all dressed in beautiful clothes, with secretive masks covering their faces.

Before they reached the doorway, Sylvie handed out

the masks from a cloth bag, then stuffed the bag into a sparkly clutch.

When they pulled the masks on they were transformed. Flora gasped. Suddenly, they didn't look like her friends any more; they were Italian aristocrats, will-o'-the-wisp creatures glittering in the evening light. The air smelled crisp, the first hint of frost on its way. It was a night where something, anything might happen.

'Piotr and Flora, you go in with the invite,' Sylvie said. 'We'll wait by the atrium emergency exit. Let us in once you're inside.'

All around them other guests were arriving, men in black or white tails, women in rainbow fabrics, swirls of motion and magic, even one or two other children, brought by their parents All of the guests had faces hidden by masks. Flora's heart felt full as she took the white card Sylvie held out and moved towards the door with Piotr at her side.

There was a huge man at the door, with a young woman beside him wearing a cat mask. She held a clipboard. He held a sense of menace. The woman checked their invite, then, with a warm smile, waved them inside.

The foyer had been enchanted.

Gone was the office look of a few days ago. Threads

of lights festooned the walls. Red and silver balloons garlanded the corridors. Music, a brass band playing fast dance tunes, called to the new arrivals. Gold signs hung down from the ceiling saying PARTY THIS WAY.

The door between the reception and the offices was pinned open and a waiter stood there, holding a tray of drinks. He wore a simple black mask across his eyes. Piotr and Flora helped themselves to juice, though their masks made it hard to drink. 'Follow the corridor,' the waiter said. 'The party is in the atrium.'

They moved with the crowd, along the main corridor, following the music and the golden signs, until they reached the party. The glass roof reflected the spinning lights of the disco ball back on to the bodies below. Everyone was splattered with moving red and blue and green patterns, like disco leopard print. The guests stood in groups, their faces hidden, heads leaning closer to talk and laugh. Some people were dancing in front of the stage, where the band kept up a loud, insistent tempo. There were more young women in cat masks holding trays of wine glasses. Young men in bandit masks circulated with trays of tiny portions of food. There were screens hanging from the ceilings, but they were dark, as though someone had forgotten to switch them on. The spook had got what he wanted – Anna's video wouldn't be on display to the crowd tonight.

A tall man with a gorilla mask was wandering through the crowd, stopping to peer into partygoers' eyes. Flora recognised the shape of Wendell Shtick. The private investigator was at the party.

She nudged Piotr and pointed him out.

'This way,' Piotr said, heading away from the gorilla-faced PI. They were shorter than everyone else. Flora's eyes were level with elbows, stoles, shawls and suit sleeves. It was a blur of bodies as she followed Piotr. Wendell was out of sight in seconds.

Until.

Ouf.

She walked right into him. He'd appeared from nowhere, and she went china-mask first into his gut. He doubled over, clutching his middle.

'Oh, sorry!' Flora gasped. Piotr glanced back. Forced to stop.

Wendell was staring her right in the eye.

He stood up. 'That's all right, miss,' he said.

Flora couldn't believe it. Wendell didn't recognise her. Despite the flaming red hair that framed her mask. He was all kinds of incompetent.

Flora was about to move off and get as far away from him as possible when he reached out and tapped her arm.

Had he lulled her into a false sense of security? Was he about to have them thrown out?

'I don't suppose you know what mask Anna van Gulik is wearing, do you? Do you know Anna?'

Flora shook her head vigorously.

'Shame,' Wendell said from behind his gorilla mask. 'I had thought she wouldn't be able to resist the lure of a masked ball. I thought maybe that was her?' He pointed to a six foot tall, skinny man in a beaked mask, whose beard was clearly visible beneath his beak.

'No,' Flora managed to squeak, her voice as high as it would go. 'I don't think that's Anna.' She thought back to the frightened, sorry Anna in her hotel room, worried that she'd ruined everything. It didn't seem likely that she'd be at the party. 'Good luck with your hunt,' she added. But Wendell was already walking away. He really was a terrible detective, Flora thought.

'*Daniel Hampshire . . .*' The whisper came from Flora's left. She spun around, to see who was talking about Dad. There were so many people, but the masks hid their faces.

'*The board is in the meeting room now . . .*' A different

voice. She turned right. Again she couldn't tell who had spoken. It was horrible not being able to see the expression on anyone's face. It made everyone seem so secretive, and sinister. As though wearing a mask was a way to keep emotions hidden, real feelings concealed. It was what the spook had been doing for a long time. Showing a false face to the world while keeping their real self hidden. Well, it was time to take off their mask.

'This way,' she said, leading Piotr to a side corridor, where a hanging green-man sign indicated an emergency exit.

Flora pushed down on the metal bar that ran across the width of the door. With a rush of freezing air, the door opened.

'About time,' said Andrew's voice outside. 'I'm colder than an ice cube on a ski slope.'

Flora stepped aside to let Minnie, Andrew and Sylvie in, then pulled the door closed behind them.

First task, getting everyone in, accomplished. Now they had to complete the rest.

'The board are meeting now,' Flora said, 'in the offices above the atrium. We need to find whatever it is on that video. Right now. And take it to them before they vote at 7.30.' She checked her watch. 'We've got thirty minutes.'

'It's this way,' Sylvie said. 'Down there.' She led them away from the party, towards a dark corridor.

Flora glanced back at the dancers and the band. They all looked so happy. It was only a few days since Dad had swapped his ironed shirts for shapeless sweatpants, but already they were starting to forget him. It sent slivers of glass into her heart. They meant everything to him, but he meant so little to them.

Sylvie turned right, then left, and they found themselves in the grey quiet of the admin block. There was no one around. The only light came from the green running-man boxes above the doors. It made everyone look ghostly.

Outside the communications office, Sylvie paused. There was a halo of cream light around the door frame. It shone through the glass in the middle of the door – the light was on inside the room.

Was there someone already inside the office?

Sylvie looked up at Piotr. He glanced around at the others. With his dark mask it was hard to see his eyes, but Flora thought he was asking a question: should they go in? Flora nodded and Piotr took hold of the handle. He turned it slowly and pushed open the door.

There was a hurried clatter from inside the room,

someone moving something quickly. Piotr rushed in, Flora and the others right behind him. In time to see Tony pushing closed a drawer on Anna's desk. He froze as he saw the gang. His mask was pushed up on his forehead, so Flora could see his guilty look clearly. 'What are you lot doing here?' he said.

'We could ask you the same thing,' Piotr replied. 'What are you doing at Anna's desk?'

'Oh, is this Anna's desk?' Tony asked with a shrug. 'I needed some paper clips, so I came in here.'

Flora looked at the desk. There were no loose papers, nothing at all that needed to be clipped together. The whole desk looked suspiciously bare.

Tony followed her gaze. 'Did I say paper clips?' he laughed. 'I meant Post-it notes.'

They stared at each other in stony silence. Not for one minute did any of the children believe Tony. His lie was as clear as cling film.

'What have you taken from Anna's computer?' Flora said, her voice as hard as steel. 'What are you trying to hide?'

Chapter Twenty-Five

Tony stepped away from the desk. He held his empty hands up. 'Nothing!' he said. 'I'm not trying to hide anything. I swear! I couldn't even log on; it's password protected.'

Flora moved to the computer and wiggled the mouse. The dark screen lit up, and sure enough, the password box was empty. Tony hadn't been able to access Anna's files.

'Sit over there,' Flora said to Tony. She pointed at a chair one desk along. Tony looked embarrassed to be told off, but he shuffled over to the chair and sat.

Andrew and Minnie moved closer to him, one on either side, keeping a close watch on his movements.

'I didn't do anything, I swear,' Tony said.

Sylvie sat in the chair Tony had left empty and typed quickly. The password was accepted and the folders and icons appeared on screen. She looked at the most recent items list – the things that Anna had been working on before she left. There were fifteen files. Some documents were easy to work out – party guest list, catering menu, that sort of thing. One was a video file. Sylvie clicked to open it. An error message popped up: *File Not Found*. The next four files were picture files: Partners 1, Partners 2, Partners 3 and Partners 4. She clicked on the first one. The same message: *File Not Found*. She clicked on the next one, and the next, and the last. All brought up the same error message. Files not found.

'Someone has deleted the video and pictures of the partners from Anna's computer,' Sylvie said.

They all turned to look at Tony.

'It wasn't me,' he said. He held up his hands. 'I couldn't even get past the password!'

Flora felt a pressure growing in her chest. An anger building. She'd hoped so much that they'd find the clue they were looking for, to save Dad from losing Breeze. But whatever it was had already been erased.

'How could you do this to Dad?' Flora said, in a voice that was almost more sob than shout.

'Do what?' Tony asked.

'Betray him,' Andrew said, leaning in as menacingly as

170

he could. Which, with the hooked nose of his masked face, was pretty menacing indeed. 'You took the blue-prints for the Breeze 5000 from the safe. You took them to the Chaussette d'Or and handed them over to Xander Drill. You blackmailed Anna to get rid of the evidence. All for money. How much did Xander pay you? How much? What was on those files you deleted?'

'What?' Tony gasped. 'I didn't! I wouldn't! I couldn't! I love Breeze and everything we've made here. It's the only good thing in my life.' He pushed up his mask further and rubbed at the red line that had formed on his forehead. His skin looked clammy, sweaty.

Flora watched his every move with suspicion. Her body language books said that people often had a 'tell' when they were lying – a specific twitch or tiny action or glance that betrayed the fact they weren't telling the truth. Did Tony look as though he was lying?

She didn't know.

'Listen,' Tony said, more softly, 'I know I might play the fool sometimes. And I definitely don't turn up for work as often as I should. But I love this place just as much as your dad does. Why would you think I'd do such a thing?'

'You're left-handed,' Piotr said simply.

'What?'

'The waiter at the Chaussette d'Or saw a left-handed person handing over a file to Xander Drill,' Andrew said.

Tony rubbed his face again. Was that his tell? Or was his mask just a bit uncomfortable?

'Flora,' he said softly, 'I've been at your dad's side every step of the way. I invested in his ideas back when no one thought they'd amount to anything. We've been together through thick and thin: when your mum left, every hospital visit Sylvie had, every school prize you won, I've been there for Daniel. I would never hurt him. You have to believe me.'

'Well, what were you doing with that?' Flora pointed at the computer.

'I hadn't even logged on!' Tony said.

'Why were you trying to log on?' Piotr asked.

'Oh, this is just embarrassing. It makes me sound so soppy. Fine! I'll tell you. I wanted to know where Anna is. She's disappeared. I wanted to find her for Daniel. Your dad is a mess without her. He's gone to pieces. He needs to fight if he's to keep Breeze. We all need him to fight. And he won't do it without her. I swear, I was just looking for Anna.'

Flora leaned against the side of the desk, letting the wood dig into her waist. She felt her eyes sting. She pushed up her mask and rubbed her eyes. She felt Piotr's hand on her shoulder, squeezing gently.

'Someone deleted that video and those photos,' Piotr said. 'They did it for a reason. We'll find out who it was, Flora, I promise we will.'

'How?' Minnie snapped. 'The board are voting soon and all of our leads just dried up.'

'Photos,' Sylvie said.

'What?'

'Photos.' Sylvie pulled open a desk drawer. She rifled through the stationery. Slammed it closed. Opened the next one. And the next. 'Photos!' she said, louder.

'Sylvie!' Flora stood upright. 'What are you doing?'

Sylvie was pulling staplers aside, turfing over hole punches, knocking aside boxes of rubber bands.

'Sylvie!'

'It isn't here,' Sylvie said.

'What? What isn't there?'

Sylvie pushed her mask up on her head and dropped to her knees. She was pulling everything from the back of the drawers, desperate to find whatever it was that was missing.

'There was a folder,' she said. 'I saw it before. A folder of photographs with a smiley face on it.'

'Photos of what?'

'I don't know, I didn't bother looking. But maybe they were the originals of the missing photos from the computer. They've been taken too.'

Flora felt a small, tiny surge of hope. The clue had been deleted from the computer, but maybe they could still find the originals. If they hadn't been destroyed.

Just then, there was a disturbance in the doorway, someone rushing in. Someone without a mask, who looked angry, furious, determined.

Anna.

Chapter Twenty-Six

'Anna!' Flora said. Anna looked wild. Dressed all wrong for a party, in her old jeans and a sloppy top. Her hair was pulled back any old how.

'You!' Tony said, from the chair where he was still under guard. 'You're back!'

'Wendell is looking for you,' Piotr said.

'I know,' Anna said in an out-of-breath voice. 'I saw him. He tried to grab me. I ran away. He's probably after me now. But I didn't betray Daniel, I didn't.'

'I believe you,' Flora said. 'But why are you here?'

'And what were the photos in your desk?' Sylvie added.

Anna looked flustered, not sure which question to answer. Then she spoke quickly. 'I came to find Daniel. I need to tell him the truth. If I'm honest with him, then there's nothing the blackmailer can use against me.

I heard on the news that the board was meeting to vote Daniel out and I couldn't let him go through that on his own.'

'You're going to tell him why you were here the night the blueprints were stolen?' Sylvie snapped.

Anna gave a tight nod. 'But I can't find him. It's these stupid masks! I can't tell who anyone is.'

'No, it's not the masks,' Flora replied. 'He's not here. He wouldn't come. He's barely got out of bed since you left. He needs you, Anna. He's a mess without you.'

'That's true,' Minnie said. 'I think he's stopped cleaning his teeth.'

'Oh. He's at home? I have to go and get him. We have to fight this together. I should have been honest from the beginning. I'm going to go and be honest now.'

Anna spun on her heel to leave.

'Wait!' Piotr shouted. 'The pictures, what were they?'

Anna frowned. 'What pictures?'

'There were photos in a folder, you had them in your desk drawer. And on your computer. But they've been deleted. And the originals are gone,' Flora said.

'Oh, those.' Anna glanced at the door. Flora realised she was desperate to get to Dad. 'They were just pictures of each of the partners from their school days. You know, in those whole-year photos that they make everyone do? I was going to use them in the video I was making for tonight.'

'Where did you get them?'

'School archives,' Anna called over her shoulder as she disappeared out of the door.

She was gone.

Flora grabbed the door frame and peered into the corridor, but Anna was already vanishing into the darkness. She was going to find Dad. Flora was pleased – Dad needed her – but Flora had needed her too. What was in those photos that had made the spook turn blackmailer?

'Can we try and find the pictures again? Maybe the schools have an online archive or something?' Andrew said doubtfully.

'We don't even know which schools they went to,' Piotr said.

'There's no time,' Minnie added. 'Anna had been working on the project for months. We've only got twenty minutes.'

Flora stepped away from the desk and sat down heavily in an office chair. It swung gently beneath her. Minnie was right. They had no time left. The vote would happen.

Dad would lose Breeze. The spook would get away with it.

She looked at Tony, still sitting in the chair opposite. She'd been so sure he was the spook. He was the only left-handed partner. Had Kamila been wrong?

Piotr was looking at Tony too. 'Do you know what schools the partners went to?'

Tony gripped the armrests as though he was about to stand up. Minnie stepped towards him and he settled back down again. 'Piotr asked you a question,' she said coolly.

'Schools? Well, I went to my local high school. I have no idea about the others. Bruce went somewhere posh, I think, but I don't know what it's called. One of those schools that does rugby instead of football and has fancy mottoes.'

'Mottoes?' Piotr said thoughtfully. '*Nihil perpetuum.*'

'You know we can't speak Polish,' Andrew said. 'Apart from *cześć* and *dziękuję.*'

'It wasn't Polish,' Piotr said. 'It's Latin. A motto. I read it somewhere. I can't think where.'

'Concentrate. Think,' Flora said. She had that excited, prickly feeling she got when cases moved up a gear.

'I can't remember.' Piotr tugged at his own fringe, as

though that might loosen the memory free. 'For some reason, it makes me think of custard.'

'There was custard on a tie!' Minnie said. 'On Bruce's tie!'

Sylvie turned back to the computer and started typing quickly. Her spelling was a bit erratic, but on the third go, she'd found it. 'Northdene!' she said. 'Bruce was wearing a tie with the Northdene school motto on it!'

A small explosion went off in Flora's mind. She remembered the research she'd done only a few days ago. About Xander Drill and his past. 'Xander went to Northdene,' she said. 'It's really posh and really strict. Do you remember what Kamila said about her Polish school? They were so strict they made left-handed people write with their right hand. Maybe Northdene is the same?'

They looked at Tony.

He looked back.

'Well?' Flora said. 'Is Bruce left-handed or right-handed?'

'I think he's ambidextrous,' Tony whispered.

'Amber Dexter?' Minnie asked. 'Who's she?'

'Ambidextrous,' Tony said again. 'It means he can use his right or his left hand to write.'

'Ambidextrous,' Minnie said, clearly liking the word.

'*Bruce*,' Flora said. '*Bruce* is the spook. He stole the blueprints. He gave them to his old school friend. He deleted the photographic evidence that was supposed to go up on the big screens tonight. He blackmailed Anna so that she would stop working on the video. We need to find Bruce and get the evidence back.'

But where, in all the swirling, whirling party mayhem, was Bruce?

Minnie checked her watch. 'The board votes in fifteen minutes,' she said. 'Then it's all over for your dad.'

'Come on!'

Flora raced out of the office, back along the corridor to where the sound of the band throbbed and echoed off the walls. Disco lights were salt-shakered over the walls as they ran out of the darkness.

The party was in full swing.

And somewhere, in the crowd of masks and dancers, was Bruce. The man who'd threatened everything.

They had fifteen minutes to find him and the proof of his link with Xander.

'This way,' Piotr yelled, and grabbed Flora's arm. 'Let's try his office.'

They surged through the crowded atrium, towards the workshop corridor. They were all there: Piotr,

Sylvie, Flora, Andrew and Minnie, and, still tagging along behind, Tony.

Piotr pushed open the double doors that led away from the music and the colour and movement of the party and into the darkness beyond.

Chapter Twenty-Seven

The long corridor was still and silent after the rumpus of the party. Its meagre emergency lighting threw a sickly glow-worm light across their masked faces.

Flora swallowed hard. If Bruce was down here, like some spider at the centre of his web, then they had to be careful. He had betrayed his friend and blackmailed his colleague. Who knew what he'd do if he was exposed now?

They walked forward cautiously. Their footsteps echoed despite their careful tread, the noise bouncing up into the concrete shadows.

Eventually, the corridor ended at the next set of doors, and the lobby.

Flora and Piotr peered through the glass into the workroom. The machines were dark. Their silhouettes stood out in the gloom like miniature cranes – all angles and elbows. Piotr pushed open the door softly. In the lobby, the cold air tasted acrid, of burnt metal shavings, solder and sweat.

Piotr held up a finger to his lips, just visible in the shadow cast by his mask. Flora nodded. They had to stay silent.

They stepped into the deserted workroom.

Flora scanned the space. It feel abandoned, empty. It was only them, and Tony, in the darkness. She hoped her guess about Bruce was right, and Tony was innocent. She eyed the tools warily.

'This way,' Minnie hissed. She crept up to a door. The plaque was too indistinct to read, but Flora assumed it was Bruce's office.

Minnie held up her hand. They all froze. Flora could hear something now. Footsteps, inside the room. Pacing. Someone waiting impatiently for something important to happen.

She turned the handle and threw open the door.

Bruce.

He was lit only by a desk lamp, which threw a huge shadow up the wall behind him.

At the sound of the door, Bruce and his shadow leaped in fright, like a spider caught red-handed.

Then he laughed nervously. 'What are you doing here? The party is the other way.'

'We know,' Flora said. 'We know everything.'

'Everything?' Bruce asked fearfully.

'Well,' Andrew conceded, 'not everything. But a lot! And we know about you blackmailing Anna.'

They were all in the room now, crowded in the doorway, fanning out around the frame.

'Wait!' Sylvie said. 'I know you! You were crying in the cleaning cupboard the day the news of the theft broke! You told me to leave you be.'

Bruce glanced around. There was only one way out and they were blocking it. 'I don't know what you're talking about,' he blustered.

'Yes,' Sylvie insisted, 'you do. That was just minutes before someone sent a horrible email to Anna! You were in that cupboard, on your phone, trying to find somewhere quiet to send a nasty, spiteful email! Weren't you?'

Bruce didn't reply. Instead, he dived for a clear vessel on his workbench. Flora had time to notice an inch of blue liquid swirling inside it before Bruce threw it to the ground. It exploded with a shatter of glass and a susurrating hiss. Instantly white mist billowed towards them. Tony dived for an extinguisher that was on a far wall.

Piotr rushed to help him. Andrew and Sylvie pulled at each other, trying to evade the mist. Flora and Minnie took the full brunt; they were closest to the workbench. It seared Flora's throat, making her hack and cough, and she doubled over. Minnie tugged her down. They both had their heads near the ground, where the mist was thinner.

She clawed at her mask, pulling it free.

Flora felt as though her lungs might burst.

The roar of the extinguisher came not a moment too soon.

She breathed again.

Then, from behind her, she heard the door slam and a key turn in the lock.

In the confusion, Bruce had lumbered past and locked them inside!

White foam was sprayed all over the workbench, but whatever it was that Bruce had set off was no longer smouldering.

'Are you all right?' Minnie said, helping her up.

Flora's throat still felt prickly, but she nodded. The others had lifted their masks too.

'What was that?' Sylvie asked.

Tony shrugged. 'Bruce has got pretty much free rein

to do what he likes in here. I imagine that was something of his own devising.'

Andrew marched over to the door and rattled the handle. The door didn't budge. He looked back at the gang. 'It's locked,' he said. 'Now what are we going to do?'

Chapter Twenty-Eight

'We need to find a way out,' Tony said.

There were no windows. The grey walls were plastered with illustrations of machines, with shelves of books and journals, but there were no gaps at all, no breaks in the solid brickwork.

Tony joined Andrew at the door. They both tugged and yanked at the door handle, but with no result other than sore hands.

Minnie ran to the phone on the desk. 'I'll call for help.' She dialled quickly and waited. Then she gasped. She lowered the phone slowly. 'It went dead,' she said.

From outside the room, they heard the juddering, crunching sound of machinery moving – the workshop grinding into life.

'It's Bruce,' Tony said. 'The phones need power to

work; he must have disconnected the phone's power supply at the fuse box.'

Sylvie rolled her eyes. 'This isn't the twentieth century,' she said scornfully. Then she pulled her mobile from her clutch bag. She stared at it. 'No signal,' she whispered.

'The mobile phone jammer,' Piotr said. 'Bruce told us it stops mobiles working in this part of the building. And he's started the machines so no one will hear us yelling.'

Sylvie put her useless phone back in her clutch.

They really were trapped.

But Flora wasn't ready to give up yet. 'If we're stuck in here, we might as well make the most of it,' she said. 'Search the place! Let's see if we can find the missing photos.'

She pulled open the drawers beside the desk.

Piotr and Minnie were right beside her.

'Sylvie,' she called, 'what did the folder look like? The one you saw in Anna's desk?'

'It was brown, cardboard, boring looking. It had a smiley face drawn on it.'

'Guys,' Flora said, 'turn this place over.' It was a phrase she'd read in a crime novel once, and she was delighted to find an opportunity to use it. It meant trash the place.

Which was exactly what they did.

Piotr took books off the shelves and peered behind

them. Andrew opened boxes and rummaged through. Sylvie opened filing cabinets and flicked through the folders. Minnie upturned chairs and looked under furniture.

All looking for the folder.

'Hey!' Andrew said.

'What? Have you found it?'

'No, but I have found this!' He held up something he'd unearthed in one of the steel cases. It looked like a scooter, but with a base plate made from reflective material and a small box near the handlebars, no bigger than a matchbox, which held a motor.

'The Breeze 5000,' Andrew said, reading the tag inside the case. 'Or at least the prototype.'

So this was the thing that had caused all the trouble – the invention that Xander Drill wanted so badly.

'It's a shame we can't have a go on it,' Andrew said, 'but this room is too small. And a bit messy.'

Flora looked at the sleek metal, the aerodynamic grips – it did look like fun on wheels. But they had a job to do, and playing wasn't part of it.

'Put it back,' she said, 'and keep on looking.'

Andrew swung the scooter around, but he couldn't make it fit back into the case. He jammed harder.

'Careful!' Flora went to give him a hand.

As she helped Andrew lower the prototype back into its protective case, she paused. The black foam, with the shape of the Breeze 5000 neatly cut into it, bulged slightly. It didn't quite fit the box. And considering Bruce was a precision engineer, that was very strange.

She tugged at the black foam.

It came away in her hand.

Revealing a brown folder hidden inside the case, with a smiley face on it.

She put the foam down gently and lifted the folder. She walked to the workbench, avoiding the extinguisher foam, and laid the folder down. She flipped open the brown cover. On top was a school photo, lines of children in blazers and caps ranked in rows. And there, in the centre of the photograph was a very young Bruce Harvey.

'Look at the boy beside Bruce!' Andrew said. 'He's got a nose that looks just like a parrot's beak!'

'Xander Drill,' Flora whispered. She remembered the one grainy photo they'd seen on the internet. Here was the same person, years earlier. Anna hadn't noticed the person beside Bruce in the photo – why would she? Drillax was a bank, as far as she knew. It was only after the theft that this school photo became dangerous. This was the evidence that Bruce had needed to bury – proof that he and Xander knew each other, and knew each other well.

She showed it to the others. Bruce's office was in a state, but they had found what they needed.

'Now we just have to show this to the board and they'll know Bruce has been lying all this time.'

'Right,' Andrew said, looking at the door. 'There's just one problem. How are we going to get out?'

Flora scanned the room again, and grinned. 'Health and safety.'

'What?'

'Health and safety.' She pointed up at the ceiling. 'Health and safety regulations stipulate that all ceilings in public buildings should be designed to be non-flammable. The most efficient way to achieve that is to create a suspended ceiling of fire-retardant tiles. Like this one.'

They looked up.

The ceiling was a chequerboard of white and grey tiles, each one a shoulder-width square. They looked so ordinary, so innocent, so perfect. So they had a way out. If one of them was willing to climb up into the ceiling.

'How do you know these things?' Andrew said in wonder.

'You pick things up when you read.'

'I read!' Andrew said.

'*Hello!* magazine doesn't count,' Minnie replied.

'It had better be you, Flora, you're the smallest,' Piotr said, focused back on the ceiling tiles.

'Well,' Sylvie said, 'we're actually identical. So we're both the smallest. But she can go. There's bound to be spiders.'

Flora wasn't bothered by spiders. But she was worried that the tiles wouldn't be able to hold her. They weren't meant for climbing on. But if they were going to help Dad, then she would have to take that chance.

Tony stood on the workbench and stretched up to the ceiling. He was just about able to reach one of the tiles with the tips of his fingers. He stood on tiptoes and managed to raise the tile a centimetre or two. Stretching as far as he could, with every muscle in his sides straining, he toppled the tile. It slid into the room, bounced off the workbench and landed on the concrete floor with a heavy crack. It split in two.

'Don't think about the concrete,' Minnie told Flora in her calmest voice.

Flora climbed on to the workbench, stood in Tony's cupped hands and launched herself into the crawl space between the tiles and the ceiling.

Chapter Twenty-Nine

Flora was up inside the ceiling space. She had to stay on all fours; there wasn't enough room to lift her head. She rested, ever so gently, on the white tile beside the hole she'd come up through. She could feel it bend, like a soft biscuit, under her weight.

It wasn't going to hold.

She was going to smash through the ceiling, falling four metres on to solid concrete.

She felt her palms slick with sweat.

She tried to take a very slow breath, but the longer she stayed still, the more the tile moved.

'The runners!' Tony said from below. 'The tiles rest on runners.'

She looked left and right. She saw what he meant. Metal strips ran in horizontal rows from wall to wall. The tiles rested on the strips. She widened her arms so her hands were off the tiles and on the metal. It immediately felt stronger. Though the edges pressed painfully into her palms.

She allowed herself a glance around. Although the space she was in was low and cramped, it was very wide. It ran off in all directions, including over the workshop! She'd been right: the tiles covered a hidden ceiling.

All she had to do was crawl so that she was beyond the wall, then drop down and let the others out.

Flora inched her way towards the clattering noise of the machines. The crawl space was thick with dust, and cobwebs brushed the bare skin of her arms with creepy tenderness. She wanted to scream and bat them away, but one false move would see her plunging through. Her dress bunched around her knees, scraping the metal.

She would have to keep crawling, and explain the ruined dress to Wendy somehow.

Every time she moved her arms and legs, she felt the runners move too. She was too heavy for them. She had to do this quickly. Flora sped up. She could see the partition wall now, which divided Bruce's office from the workroom. It stuck up like a kerb into the crawl space. She clambered over it. Now she was out of the locked room, into the workroom.

She lifted the next tile a crack and peered down.

The lights were on in the workroom. And through the crack, she could see the floor.

Way down below.

Way, way down.

If she dropped through where she was, she would smack on to the concrete and probably break both her ankles, or something equally unhelpful.

She was going to have to make her way to the middle of the room, so that she could drop down on to a table or a machine or something, to break her fall.

Flora shuffled on. The sound of the machines whirring was louder now, belts and fans, hammers and punches, clattering ten to the dozen. It was making it difficult to think.

She shoved a tile clear. It twisted in the runners and fell down. There was a crunch moments later. Flora peered over the edge. The tile had fallen on to a conveyor belt below, and was carried along until it was crushed in a die cutter.

At least the conveyor belt was rubber. It would make for a soft landing. But she would have to leap off it sharp-ish if she was going to avoid being cookie-cuttered herself.

She pulled her legs forward and sat up as much as she

could in the cramped space, above the hole. Then she let her legs drop.

There was nothing below her now; her feet kicked in empty space. Her shoe fell. She heard it crunch, seconds later, in the cutter. She held on to the ceiling runner by her fingertips.

Then let herself fall.

Her dress flipped up. She couldn't see.

She landed, hard, on the conveyor belt. Her knees buckled and she rolled on to her back. A high-pitched ringing echoed in her ears. She sat up.

Then remembered the cookie-cutter. The conveyor belt was moving her closer and closer to the thudding stamp.

She shook herself, to clear the ringing. Then leaped off.

Only to find her dress was caught on the serrated edge of the belt. She wriggled. The dress held her fast. She could feel the stamper now; the heavy thuds travelled along the length of the belt and shuddered into her bones.

Death by dress!

Not if she could help it. She gave a mighty tug and she heard the seam give way. A patch of green lace and satin ripped clear and she tumbled from the belt to the cold, hard, welcome ground.

But she couldn't rest. Getting to this side of the door was only the first part of her mission. Now she had to get everyone else out.

She stood and dusted herself down – as best she could, considering her ball dress was now the colour of a dishrag and shredded like streamers. Then Flora ran over to the locked door.

There was no key in the lock.

She banged on it. 'Are you all right in there?' she yelled.

'Yes! But hurry, the vote is due any minute,' Piotr replied.

She looked around.

The workroom was rammed with tools. There was probably the perfect lock-picking tool somewhere – a sliver of bright metal, a tiny pick, a miniature clamp.

Or a great big hammer.

She grabbed the nearest lump hammer with both hands. 'Stand back!' she yelled. The hammer wobbled worryingly as she raised it above her head. But it landed on the lock with a satisfying smack.

She lifted it again, and again. On the fourth go, the lock sheared, and the door swung open.

Piotr stood looking at his watch. 'The vote is in three

minutes.' He held out the folder to Flora. 'We'd better run.'

Flora looked at her feet. One shoe on. The other just ripped tights. 'I'll run,' she said.

'No,' Andrew replied, 'I've got a better idea.'

Chapter Thirty

Andrew held up the Breeze 5000. He swung it towards Flora with an ear-to-ear grin. 'Your carriage awaits,' he said.

Some Cinderella.

But with the clock counting down and the vote happening right on the other side of the atrium, Flora was happy to accept.

The Breeze 5000 was so light she could have held it up with her little finger. Was it strong enough to hold her? She rested the wheels on the smooth concrete floor and stepped one foot, cautiously, on to the deck. It held solid beneath her, without even the tiniest flex.

'It's got an On switch,' Andrew said, pointing to the small box on the handlebars. She flicked it. The battery indicator flashed green. The sound of a tiny motor whirred into life, like a mouse humming.

'What now?' Flora said, holding tight to the handlebars.

Andrew tucked the manila folder under her arm. 'Lift your other foot off the ground,' he replied.

She raised anchor, her right foot clearing the ground.

And the Breeze 5000 was off.

It raced across the workroom floor. Flora's hair flicked in the wind, her tattered dress flapping like sails. Piotr sprinted and pulled open the door.

She shot into the long corridor. The Breeze 5000 was almost silent as it sped along the polished concrete. A faint whir and her own rapid breathing were the only sounds. The sparse corridor windows flashed past. She caught the quickest glimpse of her own reflection, flame hair whipping out; smears of dirt – like something from a Greek play.

Then she heard the heavy sound of footsteps – the others were chasing behind her.

She gripped the bars and the Breeze 5000 seemed to respond, picking up speed. Hurtling towards the door. Too fast.

Where were the brakes?

She glanced down and saw them.

She pulled hard and the Breeze skidded to a stop.

Now she heard the sound of the party. The throb of music coming from behind the closed doors. Voices. Laughter.

She jumped off the deck, grabbed the Breeze 5000 and pushed open the doors to the atrium.

The whirl of masks on the dance floor were a kaleidoscope of reds and golds and purples and blacks; glitter and diamanté; satin and ceramic. The faces of the people were impossible to see. Was Bruce here? Flora looked around, desperate to catch a glimpse of him. Useless. There were hundreds of men in black tie and masks that might be the spook in disguise.

Flora pushed into the crowd like a rugby player into a scrum. The press of bodies was hot. Flora could hardly breathe as handbags clattered against her head, swinging elbows danced too close to her eyes. She kept a tight hold on the scooter, and the folder of photographs.

She was headed across the dance floor, towards the board meeting.

Was she in time?

Had the vote already happened?

It wasn't far now to the mezzanine floor above the atrium. The board were meeting up there.

Flora ducked her head and ploughed through the dancers until she reached the staircase.

Where a bouncer, roughly the size and shape of a cow standing on its back legs, put his thick log of an arm across her path.

'Sorry, miss, board members only.'

'I have to get through,' Flora said desperately, 'I've got to show them something.'

'Sorry, miss. I've had clear instructions. Management only beyond this point.'

Was there a way through? Could she duck past and run?

It was as though he read her mind. A quick word in his earpiece and two more cows-in-suits materialised and blocked the stairs.

'Has Bruce Harvey come this way? Is he talking to the board?' Flora begged.

The bouncer shrugged. The boulders of his shoulders strained against the fabric of his jacket.

It was no use talking to him.

Was there another way in?

Not in the time it took the board to vote.

Flora could have cried.

'What's going on?' Piotr was there at her side. The others close behind.

'He won't let me in!' Flora said indignantly.

'Well,' a voice said behind her, 'I wonder if he'll let me in?'

Flora gasped and turned. 'Dad!' she said.

He was there. Looking a bit thin and pale, but he was there. His suit looked crumpled. His mask was just a pirate hat that had come free with a burger meal. But he was there. With Anna beside him. Flora noticed her arm slipped through his. Anna gave her the ghost of a wink.

'He might let me in too,' Tony said, panting, forced to run to keep up with the others.

The cow-in-a-suit tilted his head, thinking.

Then he stepped aside.

Flora led the cavalcade of people up the staircase and into the board meeting.

Chapter Thirty-One

Ten faces turned to look at her. Shocked faces, worried faces, and one terrified face.

Bruce Harvey stood at the front of the room, before the board members seated at the polished table. Flora recognised one or two of them – including private investigator Wendell Shtick.

Bruce's white face turned ashen as he saw what she had under her arm.

'You're too late!' Bruce cried. 'The vote's been taken!'

Flora gasped.

'No,' a woman sitting at the head of the table said. 'The motion has been called, but the declaration not yet made.'

'What does that mean?' Flora looked to Dad for a translation.

He pulled himself up, letting Anna's arm drop. 'It means,' Dad said, 'that until the results of the vote have been officially declared, people are still able to change the way they vote.'

They still had time.

'Did the vote go against me?' Dad asked.

No one replied. But everyone at the table looked down, or away, or sad – it was all the answer they needed. They had voted to remove Dad.

'It's too late!' Bruce cried. 'The vote has been taken.'

'But not declared!' Piotr insisted. 'And there's something the board should see.'

Flora dropped the folder down on the table and flipped it open. She took the school photo of Bruce and Xander and threw it into the middle of the table. 'Bruce Harvey and Xander Drill, schoolfriends at Northdene Prep,' Flora said.

There were shocked gasps around the table.

'My folder!' Anna cried. 'That's why you wanted me out of the way!'

'So what?' Bruce snapped. 'You've got a photo. So I went to school with him. That proves nothing.'

Flora continued as though he hadn't spoken. 'A waiter at Xander's favourite restaurant saw a left-handed person give sealed documents to Xander Drill in a very suspicious manner.'

'I'm right-handed,' Bruce declared.

'You're ambidextrous,' Minnie said proudly.

'This is all entirely circumstantial,' Bruce said dismissively. 'Not a word of it would hold up in a court of law. Whereas Wendell Shtick has presented you with a very compelling case that through Daniel's wilful blindness and incompetence, he allowed the code to the safe to fall into the hands of the wily, conniving Anna van Gulik.'

Sylvie pushed her way to the front of the pack. 'Anna is not conniving!' she said. 'She's kind, and nice, and, well, maybe the best thing that's ever happened to Dad. And I'm sorry if I ever said otherwise.'

Anna immediately burst into tears.

Sylvie put her arm around Anna's waist.

Wendell stood up. 'The very fact that she has been in hiding all this time should lead you to conclude that Anna has a guilty conscience. I put it to you that that is solid proof that she has used her relationship to gain illegal access to valuable information.'

He sounded so pompous, and so *wrong*, it made Flora angry. 'It isn't solid proof at all!' she said hotly. 'It's proof that you're a terrible investigator!' As soon as the words were out of her mouth, Flora felt another piece of the puzzle fall into place. 'And Bruce *knew* that you were a terrible investigator when he recommended you to the partners. You told us yourself you didn't help Bruce to win his divorce case! He *knew* you were going to fail here too!'

There was a flurry of conversation around the table. Flora could pick out a word or two: 'wife took everything', 'lost his house, I heard'.

Bruce, at the head of the table, at the far end of the room, looked trapped.

'Is it true?' Wendell asked. 'Do you really think I'm a bad investigator?' He burst into tears too.

'Enough!' Bruce yelled.

The room fell silent.

'Yes!' Bruce roared. 'You are a terrible investigator! It's your fault I'm in this horrible mess. If only you had been able to find a morsel of dirt on my wife she wouldn't have taken me to the cleaners. But no, you found absolutely nothing. Zilch. So I had to go to the only banker I knew for a loan. Xander Drill. And I have come to learn that once you owe Xander Drill a favour, you are never free again. He wouldn't leave me alone until I promised to pay back the loan. I had no money; the blueprints were the only valuable thing I possessed after the terrible job this private investigator did for me! Wendell Shtick, you are the worst private investigator in the whole country. Possibly the whole world.'

Wendell bawled into his beard.

Bruce seemed to come to, to remember where he was. He looked frightened again. 'I had no choice,' he whispered, 'no choice.'

'So you gave him the blueprints?' Piotr asked. 'And you blackmailed Anna to make Wendell suspect her?'

Bruce nodded once. He held his head in his hands.

'Well,' said the chairperson, 'I think we can safely say that we need to cast our votes again. All those in favour of reinstating Daniel Hampshire and calling the police at once to deal with Bruce Harvey, please raise your hands.'

Every single hand around the table was raised.

Flora felt as though she would burst. 'Dad!' she said. 'We did it! We saved Breeze for you!' She threw herself into his hug. 'We saved the thing you love the best.'

Dad held her shoulders and pushed her firmly away. He crouched down. His pirate hat had gone askew, but he didn't right it as he kept his hands on Flora's shoulders.

'What are you talking about?' he said softly, his blue eyes looking straight into hers.

Flora found herself feeling a bit scared. Dad looked so serious, so stern. It wasn't like him at all.

'I mean, we saved Breeze for you. You can be here as much as you want, every day . . . all the time if you like,' she stammered.

He held her gaze. 'But what if I don't want to?'

'You don't want Breeze?' Flora felt flustered, confused.

'I do, yes,' Dad said, 'but it's not what I love best. Of course it isn't.'

'Mum says it is.'

'Your mum's wrong. She is sometimes, you know. I care about Breeze. But I love you. And Sylvie. And Anna.'

Flora felt as if the air had more oxygen than its regulation twenty-one per cent. She felt light-headed, floaty.

'I know I'm here a lot,' Dad was saying. 'But that's because I want to be sure that I can take care of you all. I wasn't so sad because I was losing Breeze. I was sad because I thought I'd lost Anna. And I didn't know what you two would think of me if I failed. I was worried I'd lose you.'

'Us?' Flora whispered. Dad was worried about losing her and Sylvie? 'You can't lose us, not ever – we're your daughters.'

Dad pulled her back into a hug. 'I know,' he whispered into her ear, so softly it was like dreaming. 'And I'm so, so proud of you, Flora Hampshire.'

He held her so tight it felt that his arms were the whole world. Then she felt Sylvie's arms wrapping around her back. Then Anna stroking her hair.

And then, finally, Flora felt that they'd won.

Chapter Thirty-Two

Andrew came tearing down the water slide and somehow managed to splash everyone by turning himself into a human cannonball at the bottom.

Flora shook the drips of water off her book and tugged her towel away from the edge of the pool.

'He can't help himself,' Piotr said with a grin. 'No one is safe around Andrew Jones, not even Agatha Christie.'

Minnie was in the water too, attempting handstands. Her legs kicked up, wobbled, then toppled with a splash.

Sylvie was curled up like a cat on a deckchair.

'Ice creams?' Anna called from the concession stand.

'One for everyone, I think,' Dad said. 'Here, I'll give you a hand!' He dropped his book on to his deckchair and chased after Anna.

When he caught her, he kissed her.

The gang looked away with 'eew' noises.

'Grown-ups are weird sometimes,' Piotr said. 'Still, it's nice of them to let us come along.'

'It's not Tenerife,' Sylvie said, looking up at the glass roof of the municipal baths, with the fake palm trees and painted sandy floor, 'but Dad's needed at Breeze for just a little bit longer. It's Tenerife at Christmas, though. He's crossed-his-heart-and-hoped-to-die promised.'

Andrew and Minnie raced each other to the edge of the pool, where the others were sprawled. Minnie won by a country mile. Her wet fingertips gripped the edge. Andrew pulled up a while later and hoisted himself on to the tiles by his elbows.

'You know,' Andrew said, 'there's one thing I still don't get. Bruce saw Anna at Breeze on the Saturday that he stole the blueprints. And he used that fact to blackmail her so that she'd stop working on the video. And that meant the photo of him and Xander wouldn't come to light. But what *was* Anna doing there that night? Did she ever tell you?'

Flora and Sylvie exchanged happy smiles.

'Haven't you noticed Dad's left hand?' Flora asked. 'He's wearing a silver ring. From Anna. She'd left it at Breeze by accident. She'd been carrying it around so she wouldn't lose it. But then she left it in her desk drawer.

She can be a bit forgetful. She went to get it back that Saturday; then she went to see her parents to ask their permission to give Dad the ring.'

'Why would she need their permission?' Andrew asked.

'Because it turns out she's a bit of a romantic,' Flora said.

Andrew finally worked it out. 'They're getting married!' he squealed. He launched himself off the side of the pool in delight, spinning backwards into the water with more splashes than a newspaper front page.

Flora glanced over at Dad, who was holding hands with Anna as he stood in the queue. Dad was back at Breeze. He had a lot of work to do without his chief engineer, but he was also back in the workshop, which he loved. Tony and Janyce were taking on more now that Dad was needed in engineering. He looked less stressed, less anxious. He had even come up with an idea to make the solar scooter even lighter. The Breeze 6000 was looking brilliant.

And the courts had stopped Drillax's version once Bruce had confessed to the police.

Dad's job was safe.

Which was good, because Wendy had been furious

about the state of Flora's dress when they took it back to Wardrobe. Dad had had to promise to buy imported silk to make up for it.

And now they were going to be bridesmaids.

They were often bridesmaids, for lots of extended family. Twins looked good in wedding photos.

But Flora thought she would really enjoy being Anna's bridesmaid.

She folded down the corner of the page – she was only halfway through, but she had a pretty good idea of who had committed the crime.

Then she jumped into the pool with the others.

Read on for some
top-secret character stats
on the Marsh Road
investigators!

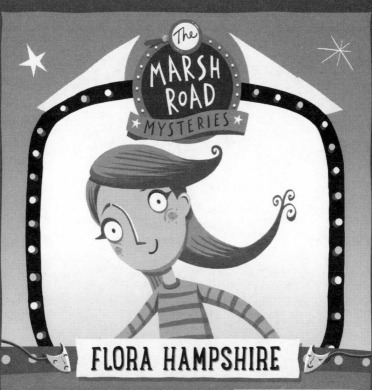

FLORA HAMPSHIRE

Good things come in small packages, and there are few people as good as the youngest twin (by five minutes) Flora. She's always ready with a kind word, or a helping hand, or a disgusting fact if that's what the situation calls for. Her book of forensic science is never far from reach. And her note-taking is the very best in the business.

Brain power:	**10**
Friendship factor:	**9**
Honesty:	**9**
Bravery:	**6**
Sleuthing:	**9**
Self-confidence:	**4**

SYLVIE HAMPSHIRE

The older of the two twins (by five minutes), Diva is Sylvie Hampshire's middle name. As a promising young actress, she demands the limelight. She'd rather be making waves than making friends. As long as her blood sugar is fine, there's nothing that can stop her getting to the top. It's been that way ever since Mum and Dad split up.

Brain power: **7**

Friendship factor: **3**

Honesty: **4**

Bravery: **9**

Sleuthing: **6**

Self-confidence: **10**

PIOTR DOMEK

Somehow, to his surprise, Piotr leads the gang of investigators. He isn't sure quite how that happened – the job just landed on him. Luckily, he wasn't hurt. Now he has to put down his comic books and pick up the reins. Who knows where he might end up?

Brain power:	**8**
Friendship factor:	**9**
Honesty:	**10**
Bravery:	**9**
Sleuthing:	**8**
Self-confidence:	**5**

MINNIE ADESINA

Minnie is as tall and as prickly as the branches of a holly tree, but her heart is firmly in the right place. Once she's your friend, she's your friend forever. On rainy days, when there's no mystery to be solved, Minnie can be found treating Mum's nail polishes like magic potions. It almost counts as a hobby.

Brain power:	**7**
Friendship factor:	**10**
Honesty:	**6**
Bravery:	**9**
Sleuthing:	**7**
Self-confidence:	**8**

ANDREW JONES

The whole world is a stage, as far as Andrew is concerned, and he is the leading man. And every other role too, if he can get his hands on the script. He loves to be the centre of attention and is always ready to take a risk. In his less dramatic moments, he helps take care of his mum.

Brain power:	**7**
Friendship factor:	**8**
Honesty:	**5**
Bravery:	**10**
Sleuthing:	**8**
Self-confidence:	**9**

Look out for the next instalment of

The
MARSH
ROAD
MYSTERIES

Cats and Curses

Coming 2016

Have you read this Marsh Road mystery?

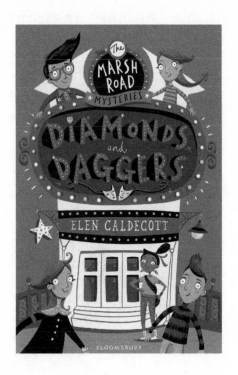

Meet the Marsh Road investigators for the first time!

Hollywood actress Betty Massino has come to
Marsh Road to star in the local theatre. WOW! But
then – DISASTER – Betty's diamond necklace is stolen!
Can the investigators solve the crime and
get Piotr's dad off the hook?

Have you read this Marsh Road mystery?

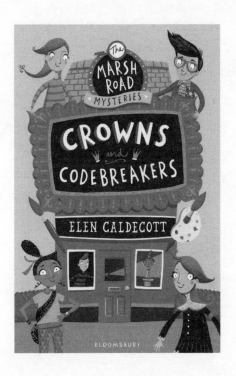

Minnie's gran comes to visit from Nigeria.
but – CATASTROPHE! – she picks up the wrong
suitcase at the airport. When Minnie's house is
burgled and the only thing taken is the case.
the Marsh Road investigators know
there's a mystery to be solved!